just one thing

Center Point
Large Print

**This Large Print Book carries the
Seal of Approval of N.A.V.H.**

just one thing

HOLLY JACOBS

CENTER POINT LARGE PRINT
THORNDIKE, MAINE

This Center Point Large Print edition
is published in the year 2018 by arrangement with
Amazon Publishing, www.apub.com.

Originally published in the United States by
Amazon Publishing, 2014.

The text of this Large Print edition is unabridged.
In other aspects, this book may vary
from the original edition.
Printed in the United States of America
on permanent paper.
Set in 16-point Times New Roman type.

ISBN: 978-1-68324-755-5

Library of Congress Cataloging-in-Publication Data

Names: Jacobs, Holly, 1963- author.
Title: Just one thing / Holly Jacobs.
Description: Center Point Large Print edition. | Thorndike, Maine :
    Center Point Large Print, 2018.
Identifiers: LCCN 2017061396 | ISBN 9781683247555
    (hardcover : alk. paper)
Subjects: LCSH: Artists—Fiction. | Bartenders—Fiction. |
    Large type books. | GSAFD: Love stories.
Classification: LCC PS3610.A35643 J87 2018 | DDC 813/.6—dc23
LC record available at https://lccn.loc.gov/2017061396

To Katie, this one's for you!

*Sometimes healing begins
with one step,
with one friend . . .
with just one thing.*

Chapter One

It was a Monday. I finished my day's work, fed Angus, and headed for the bar.

I went to The Corner Bar every Monday.

Why Mondays?

Well, Fridays and Saturdays were for dates and desperate people looking to "hook up" with others. I wasn't dating, nor was I interested in hooking up. Sundays were for church, and it seemed wrong to go to a bar that day, even though I wasn't attending church anymore . . . God and I weren't on speaking terms. Still, no bars for me on Sundays.

Midweek was filled with work around the cottage.

So, Mondays were my day.

I spared the briefest glimpse in the mirror as I left and couldn't help but notice the grey hair that had started to weave its way through the darker strands. I fingered one particularly wiry piece, thought of plucking it, but in the end, I let it fall back in place.

I walked the mile down the long dirt road to Mackey Hill, a tarred and chipped country road, then down it another mile to Lapp Mill.

The people in town said that if you blinked

as you drove through Lapp Mill, Pennsylvania, you could miss it entirely. Though it was home to a thriving Amish community, the northwestern Pennsylvanian town didn't get the attention that its eastern cousin, Lancaster, did. It was a small, quiet community. It didn't have a grocery store, though it did have a post office, two churches, and a bar.

I passed by the churches and the post office, then walked into The Corner Bar and sat down on my stool.

Sam, the bartender, served me a Killian's in an iced glass. He was tall with dark, shaggy hair and light blue eyes. I'd only noticed his eyes on my last visit, but the hair—I'd wanted to tell him to trim it for weeks, but I'd refrained.

"Hey, why does she get special treatment?" a regular at the other end of the bar shouted as he eyed my iced glass.

"She's prettier than you; that's why," Sam shouted back. Then he looked at me. "One thing."

"One thing," I agreed.

I'd been coming to the bar for about six months. Six months of Mondays.

The first four months I kept to myself and everyone pretty much let me be. But eight weeks ago, Sam had insisted I tell him one thing before he'd serve me my Killian's.

What was different that week? What had made the taciturn bartender change our newly formed routine? I didn't know, but I didn't argue. Telling him one thing about myself seemed easier than arguing.

I started with my name that first week. Lexie McCain.

As I got older I thought about forgoing my nickname and using my more formal given name, Alexis. Lexie seemed like a younger woman's name. A carefree woman. I wasn't that. But in the end, I kept Lexie. It's who I'd been my whole life and I couldn't change that now.

The following Monday, Sam issued the same ultimatum—one thing in exchange for a Killian's. I told him about the cottage I lived in. It was never intended as a long-term residence, but it was working out just fine.

The rest of that week I noticed things about the cottage I hadn't noticed in a long time. I noticed that the creek that had tripped merrily in the spring had slowed to a mere trickle under the summer's unrelenting sun. I noticed that there was a squeaky board on the porch. But mostly, I noticed how quiet it was at the cottage. That silence was like a balm. I reveled in it.

During the weeks that followed, I told him about Angus, my horribly ugly Irish wolfhound. I told him about the wood I'd split, preparing for the winter to come, even though it was still August. I told him about the spring at the edge of my eighteen acres. It gurgled along, even during the hottest, driest summer days, and fed the small pond. I told him about the vegetables from my garden that I froze for winter, and explained I liked freezing much better than canning.

I told him that I liked crafts—I didn't say art because I'd always thought it sounded pretentious to call what I do art. I taught art, but I'm more of a crafter. I brought Sam a small clay jar I'd made a few years ago. It wasn't one of my best works, but it was sturdy and honest and in that respect it reminded me of Sam.

I told him that I liked Guinness more than Killian's. He offered to stock a case, but I assured him bottled Guinness wasn't the same. Only draught would do. I'd stick to Killian's in a bottle.

Last week, I told him about the month I spent hiking through Ireland during the summer of my college freshman year.

And now, he waited for tonight's one-thing.

"I was twenty when I got married," I told Sam . . .

⚘

Lexie Morrow was using her sweatshirt as a makeshift blanket in the middle of the quad, cursing Robert Boyle, a fellow Irishman who was considered the father of chemistry. It hurt her heart to curse someone else who'd come from Ireland—her father had instilled a great sense of Irish pride in her from birth—but the reality of the situation was simply that the subject sucked.

Lexie had rapidly come to the conclusion that you were either a chemist, or not.

It didn't take any great insight to realize that she was not.

"This seat taken?"

She looked up. There in the dappled sunlight she saw a cute guy with dishwater-blond hair, standing. He sat down on the grass next to her without waiting for a response.

She wasn't quite sure how to react. Men didn't generally seek her out. Her mother would have scolded her for undervaluing herself, but the truth of the matter was, Lexie was ordinary. Not ugly, but not beautiful. Not rich, but not poor. Not brilliant, but not a dolt. Though at this moment, staring at this strange, cute guy sitting next to her, she felt decidedly doltish.

"What on earth are you studying that makes you growl like that?" he asked.

"Uh, chemistry. It is the bane of all things holy. And probably some unholy things as well."

The guy's hair was on the longer side and was already receding, though he couldn't have been older than his mid-twenties. "Julian McCain."

He grimaced as he said his first name. "I go by *Lee* now. I would have in school as well, but Mom and Dad shelled out for a good Catholic education and the nuns didn't hold with nick-names."

He waited, looking at her expectantly. There was nothing to do but introduce herself as well. "I'm Lexie Morrow, Lee. My mother tried to make me an Alexis, but the name just wouldn't stick. I've always thought I was more of a Lexie."

"Lee McCain and Lexie Morrow. They fit. I mean, if we got married, we'd share monograms." He laughed at himself.

Lexie couldn't help but laugh, too, though normally if someone else had mentioned marriage within seconds of introducing himself, she'd have been put off. But there was something about Lee McCain that couldn't be put off or ignored. There was something infectious about his chuckle. It dared her not to laugh, too.

"So, Julian? You're not overly fond of the name?"

He sighed. "It was my grandfather's name. I was the second son. My brother is John—named after my dad. I got Grandpa. John won the family name lottery."

He grinned as he made the proclamation and Lexie found herself laughing again. "Your parents gave him that name. There's nothing much he can do with *John*. But you gave yourself

14

the name Lee. That's a powerful thing—naming yourself is rather like charting your own destiny."

"I never thought of it like that."

"Looking at something in a new way, that's what every artist tries to do." Lexie realized that sounded rather pretentious. After all, she wasn't really an artist; she was just a college student studying art. She didn't fool herself into thinking she was the next Van Gogh. She wanted to teach kids, and inspire them to love art as much as she did.

"An art major, huh?" He scooched a bit closer, edging his way onto her makeshift blanket.

"Well . . ."

⚃

"And that was that.

"Lee sat next to me for two hours on the quad and we talked. He was the second of two sons, liked the certainty of numbers, and hadn't dated anyone seriously since his last girlfriend, the year before. We talked about my loathing of all things chemical, my love of pottery, and my plans to become an art teacher.

"Lee told me that he had a bachelor's in accounting. He was working at a local firm, but still took classes because he was working on his master's.

"And I was right. He was twenty-five to my twenty.

"He was right as well. We fit. Not just the names we'd chosen for ourselves or because of our monograms. Us.

"Two months later, I married him.

"I know it was fast and I'd throw a fit if my daughter did something like that, but I was young and in love. At the time, I believed that kind of love was invincible."

"You married a man you'd only known two months?" Sam sounded incredulous. "How'd your parents react to that?"

"They were pissed. They refused to pay for any more of my college. But thankfully, Lee and I were poor enough that I qualified for all kinds of grants.

"We lived in a small apartment two blocks away from campus. I painted the walls yellow and decorated it with thrift-store treasures.

"We were happy. Poor and busy, but really, really happy," I told Sam.

He'd listened attentively as I told him this week's story. Oh, we were interrupted on occasion by customers, but Mondays were a slow day at the bar, so there weren't too many.

"Where is Lee when you come here on Mondays?" Sam asked.

"He's no longer with me," I said simply, though there was nothing simple about me and Lee.

I'd finished my beer. Just one. I never had more than that. I never had less than that. One Killian's because Sam didn't have Guinness on tap.

"I'll see you next Monday," I said as I left the bar.

I walked back to the cottage in the early evening dusk. The sun seemed to want to hang on to each moment of the summer as much as I did.

I loved the smell of summer evenings. The air spoke of damp green things and dirt. But tonight, I caught the first hints of decay. Of plants that were done with their summer's work and ready to rest.

Rest.

The one Killian's and a long walk to and from the bar were enough that I knew I'd sleep tonight with Angus at my side.

He was a bed hog. But there was a comfort in curling up on my little corner just like I'd done since I was twenty and married to Lee.

I'd forgotten how to sleep in the middle of the bed.

That night I dreamed of my wedding day.

Lee and I eloped to city hall. It could have been a sad way to start a marriage, but we'd written our own vows. Maybe that's why I remembered the simple civil ceremony with such poignancy. Lee went first.

"Chemistry studies the structure and composition of matter and the changes it undergoes during a chemical reaction. That totally describes my relationship with you, Lexie. My life had a structure before you came. It had the same rhythm and certainty as the numbers I work with. But that changed when I met you. That day on the quad while you were cursing your chemistry class, there was a chemical reaction that fundamentally changed the reality of me. After that moment, I was no longer a man who saw life in black and white—you've shared your artist's vision and I can see so many colors and nuances in everything around me now. You are a part of me—the best part of me, Lexie—and this marriage only formalizes that."

He took my hand and slipped the ring on my finger as he whispered, "I love you, Lexie. Always."

It was a lovely memory.

A lovely dream.

Chapter Two

I got up before the sun rose the following Monday. While I no longer taught school, the need to get up and go somewhere was deeply ingrained. I'd developed a new rhythm here at the cottage.

I got up on weekdays and took Angus with me while I walked to the top of the cottage's long drive to get the paper. I went inside and read it as I drank my coffee. Afterward, I worked in the garden, or I went to the barn that served as my studio. The rough hemlock walls were dotted with prints by friends and other art I'd collected over the years. There was a potbellied stove that at this time of year got very little use, but would soon be lit daily. My pottery wheel and kiln stood in one corner and the huge, handcrafted loom in the other. In the middle of it all was a long, wide table that I could use for various projects.

I ran my fingers over the loom. Lee and I had found it while we were in Montana. He'd gone for an accounting conference for work, and I'd come along. We'd spent a day touring the countryside. Just two kid-free adults. We did all the things the kids would have whined about. We ate a long lunch. We walked through a cowboy museum.

Lee had spotted the loom at an antique store. I'd protested that though I'd once woven a rug in a college art class, I didn't know anything about weaving. I'd protested that it was too big, that it cost too much, that we had nowhere to set it up. Lee had bought it anyway and brought it here. He started converting the old barn at camp into my summer workshop. "Make me something beautiful," he'd said.

Lee had been on my mind all week, since my one-thing last week.

Thinking about him didn't hurt as much as it once had.

I wasn't sure if that was a good thing, or a bad thing. Just as I wasn't quite sure if Sam's one-things were good or bad. They interrupted my hard-won, quiet peace. They stirred up my thoughts and displaced the static I'd cultivated for the last year.

I worked at the loom all day. I threw the boat shuttle through one last time. Other than that one ill-made rug, I didn't know anything about weaving, though I'd read enough to muddle my way through. I'll confess; I liked the freedom that came with not being overly educated about its history and rules.

I studied my project for a minute. Sighing,

I covered my work. Though the barn was as sparkling clean as a workshop could be, I made it a habit of covering the tapestry, not only to keep dust off it, but also to put it to rest in my mind.

It didn't really help. The tapestry was the only project I was thinking about these days.

I ate a salad made from garden vegetables for dinner and fed Angus. He ran amok in the woods for about fifteen minutes, chasing anything that moved, and probably a bunch of things that only existed in his mind. Tongue lolling out the side of his mouth, he came back and collapsed on the braided rug in the living room where he'd sleep until I returned.

I left for Sam's.

It was a bit chillier than last week. One step closer to winter.

And winter here in northwestern Pennsylvania was long and cold.

Would I still be able to walk to Sam's? I'd driven the first few weeks I'd gone to The Corner Bar, but I'd walked ever since. It was only a couple miles. That wasn't a bad distance during the spring, summer, or fall, but maybe it would be too much when it turned cold? I wondered if I was forced to drive in the winter, would it change the feel of my Monday evenings?

I reached the weathered, cedar-clad building

and opened the door. Three tables were occupied and there was one guy sitting at the bar. I recognized him after all these weeks and nodded. I walked to the far end and to "my" seat. Sam smiled as he slid my Killian's in its iced glass to me and announced, "One thing."

"Lee and I had three children."

◗◖

"Constance, Conner, and Gracie, get off the roof." The twins were eight and Gracie was seven. The garage roof was their preferred playground, no matter how many times Lexie hollered.

Heathens.

She thought she'd simply said the word in her head, but realized she must have said it out loud because Lee laughed. "You wouldn't have it any other way."

"Maybe I would," Lexie countered. "Someone's going to end up falling off the garage and breaking something. And seriously, between the three of them, I'm on a first-name basis with all the staff at the emergency room. If I take them in too many more times, someone's going to call Children's Services. I mean, when I have to tell the nurse that a child rode her bike into a parked car, it sounds lame, even to me." Gracie still had a slight scar below her lower lip from where she'd put her tooth through it. Her face had left a slight dent in the car that belonged to one of the college kids renting the house down the block. It was a clunker and he'd said of all its dents, that one would be the most interesting. Lexie smiled as she remembered and wondered what he was doing now.

Lee laughed as he hugged her. "I used to spend my summers at my grandfather's. Grandma would let me and John out after breakfast, then let us back in at bedtime. We did all sorts of things that would have turned her hair grey, but she never asked and we never told, so it all worked out."

"I'm not sure the neighbors would appreciate me just turning the heathens loose on the neighborhood for a whole day. Mrs. Mickey, next door, already calls me every other day to complain that the kids' balls are in her backyard."

"I was thinking maybe we should buy some land and have a summer cottage. The kids could run the woods to their hearts' content and there'd be no neighbors to complain. And might I add, no very tempting garage roof."

Lexie knew her husband and so knew that glimmer in his eyes. "You've been thinking about this."

He nodded. "There's almost twenty acres I'd like to go look at. I thought we could pack up the heathens and a picnic and make a day of it."

She smiled and nodded her head. Lee looked relieved.

"Don't mention buying it to the kids," she warned. If they heard that, they'd never stop pestering about it.

Lexie packed an impromptu picnic, then herded the kids into the car.

"Mom, she's not bringing that old thing," Constance whined.

Gracie clutched her beat-up orange blanket closer and staunchly defended its inclusion. "It's a picnic. We need blankets to sit on."

"She's right." Lexie winked at Gracie, who smiled. That was Gracie . . . smiling seemed to be her default expression. She was sitting in the center of the backseat with Conner and Constance on either side. They say twins have a natural closeness, but Lexie's two Cons always seemed to be at odds with one another. They picked and prodded until someone was screaming.

Lee used to tease that the universe had given them Gracie a year after the twins were born to serve as a buffer.

He drove about a half hour from Erie through the small, picturesque town of Waterford, with its small shops and statue of George Washington. Then through the town of Lapp Mill up a long hill. From there, he drove on a winding dirt road, dust plumes kicking up behind the van. Light filtered through leaves. Farmhouses and fields dotted the landscape. They passed an Amish buggy, much to the delight of the kids. Conner

24

asked if they could trade in the van for a buggy. Connie told him he was stupid. Gracie pointed to a field of cows and distracted the twins from their potential fight.

Lee pulled over on the dirt road in between a stand of pines and a field that was dotted with weeds and wildflowers. He opened the door and looked out into the field. "Here it is."

Lexie got out of the van as well. "You're sure this is it?" There was no sign, nothing to declare that the property was for sale.

Lee pointed to the ones on the right side. "This is mostly pine, but according to the seller, if you follow the path back, it's all hardwood farther in. The field is part of the property, too. The owner rents it out some years to neighboring farmers. There are a lot of Amish farmers out here. He didn't bother this year because he planned on selling the plot. Oh, and he said there's a barn back there somewhere. We're welcome to hike it and see what we think."

"Dad, can we get out?" Gracie called.

"You guys can go—" Lee started.

The three kids spilled out of the van and were poised to make a run for it, but Lexie stopped them. "Sunblock and bug spray first."

They obeyed despite their grumbling. She held the bottles out to Lee, who shook his head. "I'm fine."

She snorted. Despite his Irish last name, Lee

looked far more Nordic. Blond and pale. Even the slightest touch of the sun would leave him pink.

"Hey, you're the one who will burn and peel."

"We're in the woods, goof. There's not that much sun."

"We're done, Dad," Conner said.

Lee set the kids free and like jackrabbits, they bounded in all directions. That was the nature of their relationship. Lexie was the discipline, while Lee was the fun. Lexie was rules and routine, while Lee was unpredictable. She didn't mind most of the time. It worked for them. Their marriage had weathered time nicely, despite her mother's dire predictions. Friends who'd married after knowing each other far longer had long since divorced, while they were still running strong. Oh, they hit tough times, like anyone, but they always made it through to the other side.

Lexie took Lee's hand, needing to touch him. "What if we lose them?"

"We couldn't be that lucky," he teased.

They could hear the kids whooping in the woods as they followed the barely-there path. It wound around the pines into a stand of hardwood trees. Tall branches canopied the woods and there, in the middle of it all, was a weathergreyed barn. "Why would anyone put a barn way back here?" Lexie asked.

"The owner said that the pines were once a field, too. There used to be a farmhouse back here somewhere."

They walked up to the barn. The doors were bolted, but Lee proclaimed the building was sound. "We could put a small cottage right over there," he pointed toward an embankment that looked down over the creek, "and clean the barn out so that you can use it as a studio. It's close enough to town that I can commute when we're out here in the summer."

Lee had it all worked out.

Lexie suspected he'd already decided to buy the place before they'd even seen it.

He talked excitedly as they explored the property. There was a small creek that meandered through it. A spring-fed pond. He rambled on and on about what they could do with all of it, hardly breathing. Finally, he wound down and left a silent space for her to interject a thought or suggestion. She couldn't think of anything to add.

When she didn't say anything, he finally asked, "What do you think, Lex?"

He waited and she tried to remember what she'd wanted to say. She couldn't think of anything, so she'd simply nodded.

And just like that, before they'd even unpacked the picnic lunch, they'd decided. Lexie loved the property. But even if she hadn't, she'd have said yes simply because Lee was as excited as she knew the kids would be.

It had been a long time since she'd seen him so happy.

◌◌

"Lee spent the rest of the afternoon searching for just the right spot for a cottage. He finally decided on the spot he'd originally pointed to up on a bluff that overlooked the creek. It was just a short walk to the barn. He was building the cottage in his head before we made it back to the road.

"The kids were so filthy we had to strip them down to their underwear for the ride home. Even then, they had to sit on a blanket."

"That's where you live now?" Sam asked. "On that property."

I thought about it. I guess I did live there. I hadn't been home to our house in Erie in months. Math had never been my strong suit—it had been Lee's. But I added up the months and realized it had been over a year since I'd been back.

"Yes. It's where I live now," I agreed. The admission felt monumental. Like Lee naming himself. I'd just proclaimed my home.

The cottage was where I lived.

I pushed back my glass and left the bar.

It was time to walk home.

Chapter Three

The week went by as weeks often do—one day after another. I moved from one activity to the next in order to stay busy.

There is an art to staying busy when there's nothing you have to do. No job to clock in at—no deadline looming. I spent a great deal of time at my loom working on a new picture in the tapestry. I did a small twelve-by-twelve-inch block. A barn, trees, and a picnic blanket to represent that first picnic at the camp. I focused on that day—that very happy day.

I remembered to walk with Angus and to make meals. Well, *meals* might be a stretch. Food. I made food. But almost every waking moment that week was spent on the new section of the tapestry.

As was my habit, I took Sunday off. Not that I went to church. But I took a long walk through the woods with Angus and tried to remember a time when we'd all been happy here. Images from that first trip were somehow easy to recall. The kids talking excitedly about the bridge they'd made across the creek by tossing rocks in a line. About the salamanders and water bugs.

Other moments kept trying to creep in. Moments when Lee and I fought, or worse, moments when Lee and I stopped talking. Old pains kept crowding out the happier memories.

The dog and I walked to the creek. The little stone pathway the kids had made across the water had long since washed away, but there were still large stepping-stones. I walked across them, while Angus just forded through the water, sending small fish and bugs scurrying to escape his giant paws.

It was peaceful here. My nearest neighbor was an Amish farm half a mile down the road. There was no noise from mechanical machines or loud music. Just peace and quiet.

After almost two hours, Angus and I went home. Connie called. She invited me to come visit her in Cleveland. I didn't give her a firm answer. I'd gotten very good at not really answering anyone's questions . . . except for Mondays at the bar. Maybe it was easier to talk at the bar because Sam never really asked a question. I could talk because he let me lead.

I heard the concern in Connie's voice. "Mom, I'm worried. We're worried."

I wanted to tell her I was happy, but I wasn't sure that was the truth, so I settled for,

"Honey, I'm content here. I think I'm even healing."

She sighed on the phone. It was such an adult sound, which was only right since Connie had long since stopped being one of my two Cons. She'd built her own life and that was good, but I realized that, somewhere along the line, my life had stopped.

I pondered that the rest of Sunday.

Monday came and I walked into town. As I spotted The Corner Bar, the worry that had pestered me since I spoke to Connie faded a bit.

I walked into the bar and even the scent of it felt right. Years of beers, cigarettes, chicken wings, and pizza intermingled and welcomed me as I went to my stool.

Sam slid me my Killian's. "Lexie . . ."

I waited for him to say, one thing. I had my one-thing prepared for the week. I'd tell him about the small shop I worked at in college. It was an arts and crafts store. I'd been thinking about it a lot as I worked on my piece last week.

The story was poised on the end of my tongue, waiting for him to say those two little words. Instead he asked, "Why do you walk?"

That threw me. This wasn't our normal rhythm. "You're asking a question?"

"Yes."

Just that. No explanation of why he was changing the rules of our game. And I sensed the irony in his timing since I'd just been reflecting on how easy it was to talk to him because he never really asked me anything.

I could have avoided answering tonight's question, just as I had Connie's. I could have just given him his one-thing, drank my beer, and gone home. Why did I walk?

I could try to explain it in many ways.

When I left the bar tonight, it would be dusk. Twilight. That time of night is like a soft grey blanket being laid over everything. Gently. Slowly. Until it's complete and everything is finally black.

I could tell Sam that I walked to drink in the scents. Twilight smells of silent things. Of dreams. Of hopes. Of memories.

I could tell him that I walked to listen. You'd think as the world moves over from light to darkness that things would get quiet, hushed. When I lived in the city, that's what I would have said.

Instead, there is a cacophony of sound at night. Insects buzzing. Animals rustling in the woods. Owls. Me walking. My footsteps always seem so loud. They make me sound bigger than I am, but the expanse of sky reminds me that I'm really very small.

The stars. Oh, I could tell Sam that the stars are a large part of why I walk. They're big and bright . . . not like in the city, where all the streetlights drown them out.

Those explanations were all part of the reason I walk a couple miles every Monday night here, then a couple miles back. But there was a real reason—the biggest one.

And that reason became this week's one-thing. "I walk because there, in the dark, I can sense God in the things that surround me. I can believe he's there. And I can even believe that one day, I won't be so angry with him and maybe . . ."

I let the sentence fade there, on *maybe*. It seemed like a hopeful word and it had been a long time since I'd felt hope.

I wished I'd have said all the poetic phrases that had flitted through my mind, rather than that small, honest answer I'd given Sam. But Mondays were a time for honesty and that last bit really was the biggest part of my reason for walking.

Those words should have been enough for Sam. Instead, he pressed, "Why are you angry?"

"One thing," I whispered.

"One thing," he echoed.

"It's just the first part of why. It's when the anger started . . ."

"Gracie McCain, if you don't get up you're going to be late for school," Lexie shouted up the stairs. Her youngest was the busiest of the children. Gracie was always trying to cram just one more thing into her days. Which meant that when she finally fell asleep, she slept like a rock.

And getting this particular rock to roll in the morning was hard. Getting her to move in time to get to school could be almost impossible.

"Mom," Connie whined, "Conner's so gross. He—"

This was Lexie's life and most days she was honest enough to confess, at least to herself, that she loved every minute of it. The twins were ten—a complete two-handed age that Gracie, and her not-quite-there nine, sometimes resented.

They aggravated and delighted Lexie in turn. She told friends that her kids kept life interesting. That was a curse. May you live in interesting times. She thought maybe it was a Chinese curse. Or maybe Japanese?

She was pondering where that curse originated when Lee came into the kitchen and kissed her forehead. It was an absentminded sign of affection. "Hey, honey. I've got that meeting tonight and—"

The phone interrupted Lee. Interruptions were part of their lives, but not phone calls at seven thirty in the morning. Lexie felt a rush of trepidation as she picked up the receiver. "Hello."

"Lexie, it's me." The me in question was her mother.

Marion Jones Morrow was a prominent Erie attorney who was disappointed that her daughter hadn't lived up to her true potential and become an equally high-powered something or other. Lexie had felt that disappointment keenly for as long as she could remember, but they both pretended it wasn't standing there between them. Always between them.

"Hi, Mom. What's up?"

Lee blew her a kiss and started for the door as Gracie finally came downstairs wearing what appeared to be the same outfit she'd had on the day before.

"It's your father. A stroke, they think. We're at the hospital."

It felt like the moment hung there for minutes, hours even. Lexie finally managed to call her husband. "Lee." Her voice stopped him in his tracks. "I'll be right there, Mom."

Her father? He couldn't be sick. "My dad. A stroke," she explained as she hung up the phone, snagged her keys, and started toward the door.

"Do you need me to drive you?"

She shook her head. "No, you just take care of the kids."

"Lex, I love you."

The words were the balm she needed. "Love you, too."

Erie was small enough that the drive from their Glenwood Hills home to the hospital on the Bayfront wasn't a long one. Even with the morning traffic it only took ten minutes, but it felt like an eternity to Lexie as she parked her van and hurried into the ER. "I'm looking for John. John Morrow," she told the girl at the desk behind the glass window.

A tech showed her back. And there he was—the once bigger than life, always in motion John Morrow—with her mother at his side. Lexie didn't need a fancy medical degree to see that he was gone. He was small and motionless, two words that never described her father while he was living.

Her mother looked up as Lexie came into the cubby. "They said he was gone before he got here. There wasn't a chance . . ."

Her father had always been her champion. He'd been her companion and comforter.

She remembered when she was in seventh grade—just half a step from her teens. In retrospect she realized she was already riding the wave of new hormones.

She'd come home from school, upset about . . . She couldn't remember. She simply remembered being sure that her life was over. She remembered crying to her father, in that overly dramatic way that went with the age.

He hadn't tried to tell her that everything would be fine. He'd held her and let her cry. He'd whispered, "No matter what, you'll always have me."

She looked at his body and knew that had been a lie. She wasn't ready to let him go. She still needed him. When things got bad and she wasn't sure what to do, she could always count on him to hold her and remind her that she'd always have him.

Lexie loved him, heart and soul. She loved her mother, too, but her mom pushed and prodded. She had always wanted Lexie to prove that her generation's fight for women's rights was worth it. Her father just wanted Lexie to be happy.

He'd lied. She wouldn't always have him.

He'd left her. And missing him would be an ever-present feeling.

Lexie never cried, at least not in front of anyone. Not even Lee. He'd marveled at how stoic she was when she'd given birth. How she faced everything head-on.

But as Lexie held her mother and let her cry, she didn't feel stoic; she felt shattered.

She talked to the nurse, called a funeral home and . . . It was a long, long list of things that needed to be done. Lexie did them all without shedding a tear.

She didn't even bother to wonder why.

"My father died, and I didn't have a chance to say good-bye. To tell him how much he meant to me.

"When the family got up and got ready for church that Sunday, I didn't go."

"I'm sorry," Sam said. "I know I should be able to come up with something better to say than that, but . . ." He paused as if searching for that something better, then gave a small shake of his head. "There simply aren't any words other than I'm sorry."

"Thanks," I said. I'd often wished I could come up with something better than just a "thanks" or "thank you" as an expression of appreciation, but like Sam, I'd never been able to.

"You haven't gone back to church since then?"

"No. I might have. I was actually planning to, but . . ." I took the last sip of my beer. "I'd better be going."

Sam nodded. "I understand."

I was walking toward the door when Sam called my name. "Lexie?"

I turned.

"Thank you."

I wasn't sure what he was thanking me for, but I didn't ask. That memory had taken too much out of me to care. I just wanted to walk home and nudge Angus over so I could crawl in bed.

As I reached the end of the bar, a hand snagged my wrist. "I couldn't help over-hearing," the regular at the end of the bar, who I'd recently learned was named Jerry, said. "I just wanted to say I'm sorry for your loss."

Jerry was a man on the north side of fifty. Maybe even sixty. His face was lined, as if years in the sun had left a road map on it.

"It was years ago," I said.

"Time doesn't matter when you're talking about the pain of losing someone."

Maybe it didn't, I reflected as I walked down the road toward the cottage.

I walked in the ever-darkening evening, very much aware that God was there . . . and wishing I could figure out how to reach him and wondering if I found a way to do it, would it help?

Chapter Four

I dreamed that night. It was a snow day in Erie, which meant the city schools were canceled. The twins were maybe seven, which would have made Gracie six. We built a tent in the middle of the living room out of blankets and quilts. We played there all day as the city got buried by a horrible lake-effect snowstorm. In our tent, we didn't even see the snow.

Gracie crawled on my lap and whispered, "This is a magic tent, Mommy."

And it was magic. In that tent, for that day, the rest of the world ceased to exist.

When I woke up, I could still smell Gracie's shampoo. I could hear the kids laughing. We'd all felt safe in that magic tent.

I tried to hold on to the memory . . . to the dream. But Angus nudged me, telling me it was time to wake up and feed him.

I did, but the dream left me with a lingering feeling that I needed to see the kids.

Since I moved to the cottage, I'd made it a point to call them at least once a week, but it had been months since I'd seen them in person.

Talking about losing my father had loosened

something in me. Even after I lost him, I held on to the knowledge that he had loved me.

I needed to be sure the kids knew I loved them.

I called them and invited them to dinner at the cottage. I thought about saying, "Meet me at the city house next weekend," but I wasn't quite ready for that, so I settled for inviting them to the cottage on Saturday night.

Cleveland is a couple hours away, so I told Connie that she was welcome to spend the night. She's the only one to move away from Erie. Morrows have lived in Erie for generations. It was as if that initial migration from Ireland here was all the travel the family could manage. Morrows never moved.

Except Connie. Sometimes it made me sad, but since I'd come to accept that I now lived outside Erie myself, I understood. Even before everything happened, I understood. Conner had always been my easy one. Gracie my peacemaker. Connie my restless spirit.

Maybe it was wrong to label your kids, but I don't think I chose their labels. I don't think I forced them into some niche I'd created. They invented themselves. I just understood them, or at least tried to.

I spent the Saturday making a nice dinner. I rarely cooked anymore. It didn't seem worth it when it was just me and Angus. Sometimes

I made an occasional omelet, but rarely much more than that.

At dinner, the kids caught me up on their lives and their adventures. Conner had a new girl he was seeing, but not seriously. He offered to come mow what yard I had here at the cottage, but I assured him I could manage.

After an apple crisp dessert, he headed back to Erie, which left only Connie and me. I was used to the silence when I was out here with only Angus, but it seemed too quiet with Connie here. After years when they were kids and chaos ruled, the silence was unnerving. "Would you like to go for a quick walk with Angus and me?"

Somehow being quiet outside didn't seem as bad.

"Sure, Mom."

We walked for a while. Angus flushed a turkey from some underbrush. It scared Angus more than it startled us. We both laughed at the sight of the giant dog, quivering because a turkey had flown at him.

"He does keep things interesting," I said. "This spring, he met up with a skunk. I'm not sure I told you." Connie shook her head, indicating that I hadn't. "I bathed him in tomato juice, then finally in peroxide and baking soda."

"That's a lot of dog to bathe," Connie commented.

He was. I'd bought Angus long after she'd left the house, so they were friendly, but they weren't overly attached. She'd made comments suggesting I might have been better off with a smaller dog, but there were a lot of empty spaces in my life and I figured it took a very large dog to start to fill all those voids.

"Mom," Connie said a while later.

"Yes, honey?"

"When's the last time you left the house? I mean, other than running to the grocery store or bank."

I knew that she was asking about more than if I'd become a total recluse. "I'm busy here. I've been working on a new project and it's going really well."

"Can I see it?"

No, I couldn't share the piece yet. I wasn't sure why. It had as much to do with her as it did me. But right now, I needed to be selfish, to hold on to it myself.

"When it's done," I promised. "But just to set your mind at ease, I go out every Monday night."

"Where?"

"I meet friends in town."

Now, maybe a month ago, that would have been stretching the truth to the point of being a lie, but things had changed. Mondays were no longer me forcing myself to leave the house. Somewhere along the line, I'd started looking forward to going out. And it wasn't the Killian's, though it was a very good lager. It was Sam. He'd become a friend. Telling him just one thing a week . . . it helped.

I thought of Jerry, offering me condolences. Maybe he was a friend, too.

If Sam, or anyone, had wanted to know the whole of my story, I'd crumple under the weight. But telling it in dribbles, well, it was like deflating a balloon. It released just enough that I could let it go and adjust to my new dimensions before going out the next week and letting some more out.

"A girl friend, or a guy friend?" Connie asked.

"A guy, but—"

"Friends. Is that all?" she teased.

I must have looked . . . well, I'm not sure how I looked, but Connie's teasing stopped abruptly and she said, "I'm sorry, Mom. You know, you have every right to date," she added in one fast sentence, as if she felt she'd better say the words quickly in hopes I'd listen.

"Right doesn't always matter, does it? If what was right and fair mattered, then I wouldn't be here, would I?"

44

"Mom."

Then my daughter, my beautiful daughter, hugged me. She hugged me as if I were the child and she the mother. Only my mother would never have hugged me like that. Not that she didn't love me. My mother just never knew how to show her love the way my father, or even my daughter, could.

"Would you like to know something . . . one thing about your grandmother?" I asked Connie.

"Sure, Mom."

I took her hand, this daughter of mine, and whistled for Angus. We started back toward the cottage. The woods were dark, but they were my home now and I knew the way.

Then for the first time, I shared one-thing with someone other than Sam. "I spent most of my life not knowing my mother could laugh."

❦

Lexie and her mother stood next to a large, black headstone in the middle of Laurel Hill Cemetery.

Lexie had no idea what was the proper thing to say about a headstone. "It's beautiful, Mom," she tried. To be honest, she found it disconcerting that her mother had her name and birth date already put next to her father's. All that was left was filling in the date of her death.

Lexie didn't tell her mom that she wasn't sure

she liked that part. Her mom, being her mom, would simply say that it was expedient. That it made sense.

Lexie knew her mother believed in making sense.

"I prearranged my funeral with Kloecker's Funeral Home, where we had Dad—"

"I remember, Mom." Did her mother expect her to say *thank you* for taking care of it? Lexie didn't know, and she was saved from gracelessly fumbling when her mother added, "Oh, of course. And I bought a third plot when I bought ours."

"What?"

"It was here, all by itself, so the cemetery made us—" She stopped short and corrected herself. "Me. They made me a deal. You never know . . ."

Lexie lost track of her mother's words as she spun around and walked away from her father's grave. Her father would have understood how her mother's particular brand of expediency bothered her. She'd always had a particularly rocky relationship with her mother. She was not the daughter her mother had dreamed of, but unfortunately, she was the daughter her mother got.

"Alexis. Wait for me."

So Lexie stopped. She'd have loved to just keep on going. To walk away from her mother. To quit trying to please her, when it had long since become apparent that her mother would never approve of Lexie's choices. But she couldn't. It would have broken her father's heart.

Her mother put her hand on Lexie's shoulder. "I'm sorry. I know you hate this kind of thing. I do my best to shelter you from it, but you're all I have left now. When I die, you'll be the one trying to take care of the arrangements and I wanted to make it easier on you."

"Easier on me?"

Lexie tried to tug away from her grip, but her mother didn't let go. "Alexis, I . . ." She stopped, then started again. "The kids are in school until two thirty, right?"

"Right."

"Then we have a few hours. Come down to the peninsula with me."

Lexie loved the peninsula. Presque Isle was a small spit of land that jutted into Lake Erie, creating a sheltered bay on the Erie side, and rocky beaches on the lake side.

And to the best of her knowledge, her mother had never gone there with her. Lexie had gone with her father, with friends in school, with Lee and the kids, but never with her mother. "Uh, sure."

Her mother drove with clipped efficiency down Sterrettania, which turned into Peninsula Drive, and finally drove out to Beach Five. Her mother drove past the tourist hotels and restaurants as if she came this way often.

"You've been out here before?"

Her mother turned and gave Lexie one of her famous mom-looks. The one that said, I don't know what goes on in your head. "Alexis, I've lived in Erie all my life. Of course I've been out here."

"Oh."

When her mother parked the car, she took off her Marc Jacobs heels and her trouser socks, then cuffed up her Michael Kors pants.

Lexie only knew about Marc and Michael because her mother always introduced her clothes, just as she might a colleague. "Look at my new Marc." Or, "What do you think about these Michaels?" Lexie knew her mother had probably told her the name of her blouse's designer as well, but she couldn't remember it. Designer names meant nothing to her. She spent her days working with clay and paint. She shopped generic brands, not designer names.

Ready for the sand, her mother took off up the beach.

There was nothing left for Lexie to do but follow.

Her mother walked at the water's edge and occasionally leaned over to pick up a piece of beach glass, or wave-polished stone.

Lexie expected a talk, or a lecture, but instead they walked in silence until a giant dog came barreling toward them, splashing in the leading edge of the waves.

"King," someone farther down the beach yelled.

It was too late. King honed in on her mother and practically knocked her down with his very affectionate greeting.

"Hold on, Mom, I'll get him."

"He's fine," she said, laughing. "You're fine; aren't you, King?"

Lexie stood there watching her mom, someone she'd always thought of as remote, playing with a dog in the water, ruining her designer clothes.

King's owner finally caught up and retrieved the dog, while offering her mother profuse apologies. "It's fine," she said graciously. "I love dogs."

She laughed out loud and stroked the sopping, soggy dog.

Lexie couldn't remember ever hearing her mother laugh, at least not like this. Joyful. That was the description.

She knew her mouth was hanging open, but she just couldn't seem to adjust her reality to this mother . . . this laughing mother.

After King's owner left with the dog, Lexie said, "Mom, you hate dogs."

She'd wanted a dog when she was growing up. She'd wanted one so badly. She remembered pretending her neighbor's yappy poodle was a giant Saint Bernard. *Her* giant Saint Bernard. Lexie had begged and pleaded, but her mother always told her no. Her father made her stop bugging her mother, saying that her mom wouldn't be able to deal with the mess a dog would create.

Yet, here was her mother, soaking wet and covered with dog kisses.

"I don't hate dogs, but your father was allergic," her mother said quietly. "He didn't want you to blame him . . ."

"So, he let me blame you?"

Mom shrugged. "You were always closer to your father." Before Lexie could protest, she added, "It's okay, Alexis. I know I'm not very . . ." She paused and with a small smile filled in, "Cuddly. You were five when you told me that. I knew you needed someone who was more approachable. I was always glad you had your dad."

"Mom." Lexie wanted to hug her, but she settled for simply placing her hand on her mother's very wet arm.

"You know what?" Her mother looked determined. "Your father is gone. I'm still here. And I'm getting a dog. Want to come help me pick one out?"

There was her mother. Standing up to her ankles in the water, wet paw prints on her normally impeccable outfit, and she had never looked more beautiful.

Connie grinned. "And that's when Grandma got Jazz."

"Yes. I found Bernie there, that same day."

"I remember when you brought him home. He was ugly and we couldn't figure out why you got him. But you always wanted a Saint Bernard."

"Every time I looked at him, I remembered my mother, standing in the water, laughing as a dog kissed her. He reminded me how much she loved me. She loved me enough to let me blame her for my lack of a dog growing up. She did it because she wanted my dad to remain my hero. I hadn't realized how deep her love ran then, but I know now."

Connie had tears in her eyes. "I love you, Mom. And I've never doubted how much you love me."

And Connie hugged me. I'd worked so hard to have a different relationship with my kids than my mom had with me. At that moment, I thought I'd maybe succeeded.

We walked back to the cottage and I offered Connie the bed, but she took the couch. Sometime in the middle of the night, she came in, just as she had when she was little, and slipped into the big king-size bed with Angus and me.

Chapter Five

Monday came and I set out for the bar with a different sense about the trip.

Normally, I went because it had become part of my routine. It was how I justified telling the kids I sometimes left the cottage. But tonight, I wanted to go.

I wanted to see Sam and even Jerry.

It was a beautiful evening. The sky was very, very blue, without a whiff of a cloud. In some parts of the country they talk of endless skies, but here in northwestern Pennsylvania, the sky ends abruptly at the edge of tree lines, or over the crest of a hill. Blue butted up to trees, houses, and roads. But as I stood at the top of Mackey Hill, looking down, I was high enough that I could see much farther. The sky wasn't exactly endless, but it was huge and brilliant. It seemed to match my anticipatory mood.

I smiled as I entered the bar. It was familiar . . . a haven. "Hi, Jerry," I said as I passed him and made my way to my stool.

He looked surprised, but echoed my greeting.

I took my seat. "Hi, Sam."

He smiled at me. "Hi," he replied as he handed me my beer in its iced glass.

"One thing," he said.

"One thing," I echoed almost cheerfully. "I didn't get my first dog until I was in my thirties." I told Sam about adopting Bernie, an already-aging Saint Bernard who could produce the most prodigious amount of slobber. I told him about the time we took Bernie to camp and discovered that I'd bought a dog who couldn't swim, and how Lee had to jump into the small, spring-fed pond, fully clothed, and rescue him.

Then I told him that Bernie had passed peacefully in his sleep and now I had Angus, the less-slobbery Irish wolfhound.

After that, I'm not sure why, I looked at Sam and said, "One thing?"

He looked startled. *I* had changed the rules this time.

For a moment, I didn't think he was going to respond, but slowly he said, "I was in the army."

I tried to picture laid-back Sam in the military, but I just couldn't manage it. Tall, with loads of dark hair and a killer smile. This was not the kind of man who fought in wars.

"I joined the army in the wave of patriotism

that swept the country after 9/11," he continued. "I believed we were going to stop Al-Qaeda; we were going to find Osama bin Laden and make him pay.

"What I found was Afghanistan. Colder than I imagined. And the dust. I don't think I'll ever really get rid of the feel of that grit coating my body.

"I was part of Operation Enduring Freedom.

"Six months after I got there, there was a bomb . . ."

෴

Things were fuzzy.

Sam Corner couldn't make sense of the strange shapes and noises.

It was the smell that finally started to clear his head.

Antiseptic. Strong.

It reminded him of visiting his grandfather in the hospital.

And that's when he formed his first real thought. *I am in a hospital.*

He slept after that. Sometime later, he awoke and didn't need to think in order to remember that he was in a hospital, but he did need to decide why.

As he concentrated, a rush of pain enveloped him.

That's when he realized that everything hurt.

Everything.

But most especially, his right leg.

A nurse came in. He was relieved to discover he thought she was cute.

That was a good sign.

"You're awake. I'll go get the doctor."

He waited for a tall, greying male doctor and instead got a cuter-than-the-nurse, blond pixie of a doctor. "I'm Dr. Lynne. Can you tell me what happened?"

"I was hoping you'd tell me." His voice sounded rusty to his own ears, but it worked.

"There was a bomb . . ." She talked about broken bones and shrapnel. Whatever surgery they'd done had been a success.

She talked and talked, and he tuned her out by focusing on one small blond curl that bobbed up and down as she spoke.

"How long?" he asked and when she didn't answer immediately, he repeated, "How long until I can go back?"

"Lieutenant, you're not going back."

⚭

"I bet I'll buzz when I go through airport security now," he said with a small laugh, as if to lighten the story.

Thinking about Sam in pain hurt me. "I'm sorry, Sam."

"Hey, I came home in one piece. It might be a broken and screwed back together piece, but I'm here. Not everyone in my unit came

55

back. But I did. I came home and bought the bar. And I'm here."

He said the words as if he needed to reassure himself that he was indeed here.

I understood that.

I reached across the bar and took his hand in mine. For the first time, I saw the scars traveling up under the sleeve of his denim shirt. I squeezed his hand and said, "Thank you."

There was nothing left to say after that other than, "See you next week."

I left the bar and walked home.

It was later than usual. Dusk had long since turned into true night.

Usually, the moon provided enough light to illuminate the road if I walked home later than normal, but tonight, it was barely a sliver in the sky.

I was almost home when I heard a rustling in the woods to my right.

I stopped.

In northwestern Pennsylvania, there aren't many things that can eat you. We have some bears, and there are bobcats and fox, but none of them attacked people often. Unless they were rabid.

More rustling. I stood on the berm, almost in the ditch that edged the dirt road for rain runoff.

I stood as still as I could and waited.

Then they came out.

A doe and three fawns.

I knew that deer had twins frequently, but I'd never heard of triplets. But there they were. So close I could have tossed a pebble and hit them.

I wasn't sure if the wind was blowing just right and they didn't catch a whiff of my scent, or if they knew I'd never hurt them. But whichever it was, the four of them daintily leapt over the ditch and walked across the road.

And I stood and marveled.

Sometimes, you find yourself inadvertently in the dark. But I'd discovered that if you stopped fighting against it and just stood still, sometimes something marvelous comes along.

Chapter Six

Making a tapestry differs from traditional weaving. There is no uninterrupted pattern. Instead, pictures are carved out of the warp and weft threads. Most tapestry pieces are planned to the most minuscule detail.

My piece was not traditional, mainly because other than the barest of how-tos, I didn't know much about weaving. I'd started what I thought was going to be a small blanket, more of a throw. Five foot by seven foot, a dusky blue.

I read a book about tapestry and decided to experiment. I'd woven about half a foot of my throw, and stopped and added a picture of the quad on the campus where I'd first met Lee. A swath of green with a brown bench. I tied the edges of the picture to the main piece and would stitch them together when the piece was done. Then, I made our garage, where the kids had climbed whenever I wasn't looking.

Each picture was about one foot by one foot. I decided to do a row of three. I added a picture of my father, with me on his shoulders.

Framing in the individual pictures was a

traditional weave, done in that same blue I'd started with.

The next row started with my mom standing in the water with a dog licking her face. She was laughing. Then, I did a picture of the barn and the picnic blanket.

I'd spent the week working on the deer and her three fawns. A reminder to myself that even in the darkest places there was beauty. This was by far the most involved picture. I worked until my eyes felt rough with grit and my shoulders ached from hunching over. I'd wanted to finish the square before leaving tonight for the bar and I did . . . barely.

I covered the loom and the project, then called Angus. "Here, Angus. Supper."

Angus wasn't as smart as Bernie had been, but he knew the word *supper*. He woke up and stretched. He liked to sleep on the time-dimpled old couch I kept in the barn.

"Supper," I tried again.

His tail wagged lazily. I realized that Angus was getting old and I rubbed the ratty hair on his head.

After he'd eaten, I let him outside, then waited until he'd come back in and settled on the couch before I headed to my Monday night date.

"One thing." Sam slid me my Killian's.

"One thing," I echoed. I hadn't planned

what I was going to say tonight. And I was surprised when the words "Gracie got sick when she was fifteen" came out of my mouth.

⚬

Lexie was putting away laundry.

Her friend Lucy made her kids put their own laundry away, but Lexie had found that if she did that, the clean clothes sat in piles wherever she left them and the kids just worked out of them. So, she put the laundry away herself in order to save what little of her sanity was left.

Having three teens all at once was more than any woman should cope with, especially given she was teaching art at the high school and dealing with the teens there all day as well. That was simply way too many hormones in her life.

She glanced out the back window as she tucked Gracie's underwear into the proper drawer and saw her two beautiful daughters splayed flat on the garage roof. Conner was down on the ground, looking around . . . she assumed for them.

She'd thought they'd long since outgrown the garage roof nonsense. Seriously, they were in their teens—supposedly well on their way to adulthood.

She put the half-emptied basket on Gracie's bed and stormed down the stairs.

"All right, you heathens," she hollered. "Down, now."

"They're on the roof?" Conner gave a bellow of outrage. "You two are dead," he screamed as he started to run toward the back of the garage. That's where the small peach tree they used as a ladder stood.

"That's far enough." Lexie took him by the back of the collar and walked back there. "What did they do?"

"They were spying on me." His brotherly frustration was apparent not only in his tone, but in his ramrod-stiff spine and fisted hands.

"What were you doing that their spying would upset you this much?"

"I—"

A long, tanned leg came over the edge of the garage roof and stepped onto the big tree branch.

Connie looked down at her. "Mom, he said he was gonna kill us."

"Yeah, I am," he said, confirming Connie's statement.

"No, you're not," Lexie assured him.

She turned to Connie. "He's not," she told her daughter. "But who do you think you should fear more? Your brother, or me?" Lexie tried out her best mom-glare. To be honest, most of the time, she knew she wasn't overly scary, but today she must have managed it because Connie looked nervous.

Connie jumped from the tree. "Mom, he was talking to his girrrlllfriend." She drew the word out and it set Conner off. He charged, but Lexie still had his collar so he didn't go far.

"Gracie Ann McCain, you get down here, now. And you two, just stand there and be quiet."

Gracie's right leg came over the edge of the garage, her left one followed, the leg of her pants was hiked up as she wiggled down and her calf was exposed. A huge, purplish-green bruise stood starkly against her skin.

"Gracie, what did you do now?" Lexie asked. All her kids were accident-prone. And even now, she took one or another to the doctor's for the minor injuries, and on more than one occasion to the ER. Just last month Conner had been chasing after Connie for some other outrage. He'd been wearing socks and had barreled into the corner of the doorway, practically knocking himself out. She'd loaded him into the car and headed for the emergency room for stitches for the long cut on his forehead even as he'd insisted, "Duct tape and superglue, Mom. That's all I need."

She could barely see his scar, but Gracie's bruise stood stark on her leg.

"It's that same one," she said as she slithered the rest of the way down the tree and landed on the ground next to her sister.

"The same one from a couple weeks ago?"

"Yeah."

Lexie had noticed it on one of the last hot days of summer. Gracie had had on a pair of shorts and the bruise was so big and ugly-looking it was impossible to miss.

She'd wanted to take her to the doctor's, but Lee had teased her about being an overprotective mom. He'd told Lexie over and over again that kids get bruises.

"You two." She pointed to Connie and Conner. "In your rooms and stay there. Don't touch or do anything. Just sit on your beds as if you were five-year-olds in time-out. That's how you're acting—like five-year-olds. It's time you realized that you are sixteen and way too old for this nonsense. And you"—she pointed to Gracie—"get in the car."

"Why?"

"We're going to the doctor's."

✿

I couldn't finish my beer. I just pushed back the stool and left, walking as fast as I could, tears streaming down my face.

I shouldn't have said anything. I shouldn't have started this particular one-thing. I wasn't ready for it. I wasn't sure I'd ever be ready for it.

"Lexie." It was Sam. I didn't have to look. Even if I hadn't recognized his voice, I'd have known it was him.

"I've got to go," I said, walking faster. It was almost a run.

"Lexie, stop."

I turned and Sam was hurrying toward me. He was limping. I'd never noticed he had a limp behind the bar. But now, he was coming toward me as quickly as he could and that limp was evident.

I waited at the side of the road until he reached me. He stood close enough to touch, but came no farther. "Lexie, what happened to Gracie?"

"I don't like it when you ask questions."

"I know. So, I don't do it often. But this one needs to be asked. What happened to Gracie?"

"Not yet," I said. I knew that story needed to be told, but I couldn't yet.

Sam understood and just nodded.

My fists were balled, every muscle in my body taut. I wanted to hit someone, something.

And then, Sam just opened his arms and engulfed me.

Standing at the side of that tarred and chipped road, he held me, and slowly my hands relaxed.

He smelled exactly how I'd have said Sam should smell. There was a faint whiff of beer. Maybe the hops. Cinnamon. There was a definite scent of cinnamon. Laundry soap.

He crooned words that I couldn't quite make out because his voice was a whisper, but I knew their meaning. It was fine. I was fine. He was here.

"You're angry." Those words I could make out. It was a statement. It was Sam's way of saying he understood.

I nodded against his chest.

"I get that. You didn't ask, but here's my one-thing . . . When I woke up in the hospital, I was furious. Furious at everything and everyone. My mom came every day and took the brunt of that anger. And one day, she looked at me and said, 'I only had one child, but I lost him to the war. You've changed. You're no longer the boy I knew. What we both have to figure out is who you're going to change into.' It took me a long while to figure out who I'd become. If I'm honest, I don't think I've got the whole picture of who yet."

He released me enough that he could look at me. "Who did you change into, Lexie?"

"I don't know."

"I read this book once that said we meet the people we need to meet when we're ready for them. Maybe that's why we met. To try and help each other figure out who we are now."

"Maybe," I admitted. It would be nice to think that things happen for a reason. That people come and go in our lives with purpose. Maybe there would be some comfort if I started to believe that. But I couldn't think about it anymore that night.

As if sensing that, Sam said, "I'm going to walk you home tonight."

"I don't want to talk anymore." It wasn't just that I didn't want to; I couldn't. I couldn't force another word out.

There was no room for any more words—not tonight.

"That's fine," Sam said. "We'll just walk along together, quietly."

So, for the first time, Sam walked me home. It was a long walk, but true to his word, he didn't say anything. Neither did I. He held my hand as we walked. His limp wasn't quite as pronounced at the more sedate pace.

We turned down my long, dark drive that had been tucked between the old pine trees and the field. The pines had all died now, and slowly they had been replaced by hardwood trees. I couldn't believe how big those trees had gotten. Though it was so dark I couldn't see them, I knew that they towered over where the pines had once stood.

Sam wouldn't see them, but I knew they were there. Here, hidden beneath all the trees, I'd found some measure of comfort.

"Who's watching the bar?" I asked. My voice felt out of place in the dark.

"Jerry."

"You know, you may have no beer left when you get back there." I tried to make it sound like a joke, but it fell flat.

"It would be worth it. You're worth it."

And on that note, he turned and walked back up the driveway toward the street and as he walked away, I realized something—one thing—Sam Corner had become something more than just a Monday-night friend.

Chapter Seven

I stayed close to the barn that week, working on my project. I only walked away from the loom when Angus made it clear I had to.

There was no subtlety to the dog. He'd simply grab on to any piece of my clothing he could and pull.

So, I walked and fed him when he made me. I slept when my eyes grew so bleary I couldn't see straight.

But otherwise, I worked.

I did a few more rows of uninterrupted weaving. And fingered through my wool, looking for an inspiration.

I pulled up a skein of black wool.

Now, most hand-dyed wool I've seen tends to produce blacks that are on the greyer end of the color spectrum. But this was a beautiful piece. As black as black could be. And I knew what to make.

When I got to the bar on Monday, Sam gave me my glass and said, "One thing."

I knew he thought I was going to talk about Gracie's illness, but I just couldn't yet. So, I copped out and said, "When I was five, I wanted a horse for my birthday . . ."

Lexie Morrow wanted a horse. She asked her father for a pony for her fifth birthday. Her sixth. Her seventh. She was in fourth grade when she finally realized she wasn't going to get a pony any more than she was going to get a dog.

It was the fall of her eighth-grade year when her parents took her to Cook Forest State Park and her mother took her on a trail ride. Lexie had never been on a horse and she was so excited that she could barely contain herself.

"Can I pick which one I want to ride, Mom?" she asked as they drove up to the stable.

Her mother turned around and nodded. "Yes, I'm sure you can," she paused a moment and added, "and you also may."

Lexie felt chagrined. Her mother was a champion of proper English and hated it when she said *can* instead of *may*. "Sorry."

Her father parked the car and Lexie was out the door and hurrying to the horses that were tied up along the front of the split-rail fence.

Her mother came up beside her. "So, which one?"

There was no one else at the stable. It was late in the season. The man said they were moving the horses to their winter stable the next week, so this was probably the horses' last trail ride of the year.

She looked through the choices. The muddy

white one. The bay. But it was the giant black horse that caught her eye. "That one."

"Are you sure?" her mother and the stableman asked at the same time.

"I'm sure." Lexie listened intently as the guide talked about safety. How to get on and off a horse. The fact that these horses were trained to follow one another. Even non-skilled riders would be okay.

Her mom got on her horse all by herself, but the stableman helped Lexie on. She didn't care. She'd made it. She was sitting on a horse and about to go on a ride. This was what she'd always dreamed of.

The guide got on his horse and started toward the trail. Lexie and her horse went next. Her mother followed.

Her father had opted not to go for a ride and hollered, "Have fun," as they rode by the car.

Five minutes into the ride, Lexie decided her horse, which shared the name Lucy with her best friend, should have been named Lucifer. She knew that Lucifer was another name for the devil because her mom read her a book one night that talked about Lucifer, and Lexie had had nightmares for weeks.

Lucy had a gait that was more a canter than a walk. How Lexie managed to stay behind the lead horse, she didn't know, but every step Lucy took jostled her from side to side.

Lucy kept leaning over and trying to snag pieces of grass.

The guide turned around and said, "Just give a soft tug on the reins to tell her who's boss."

Lexie did.

And Lucy was very much reminded who was boss.

Lucy was.

☙

"She took off across the field with me on her back and the guide on our trail. But that horse was fast. It felt like we ran for hours before the guide got alongside us and grabbed her reins.

"That's when I learned a lesson—what you think you want isn't always what you want at all."

Sam smiled. "You discovered you didn't want a horse?"

"That's exactly what I discovered. I was meant to read about them, but not ride them."

Sam had listened attentively, as always, but as I wound down, he looked disappointed. I knew what he'd expected and knew I had to say the words. Whatever this was on Mondays, no matter how much it hurt, I knew it was good for me. That working on the loom and talking here . . . well, it was good. I was a bit better every week.

So I reached for whatever courage I had left and said, "I pulled those books—my old horse books—out for Gracie after . . ." She let the sentence hang there and scrambled for some footing.

"She'd loved the story of my one and only horseback ride when she was small. I'll confess; I may have embellished a bit. We'd finished *Misty of Chincoteague*, though at sixteen she was far too old for it . . ."

Lexie closed the book and stared out the window at the beautiful spring sky. "Maybe when you're better, we'll go to Chincoteague. I've always wanted to see the ponies there. I want to watch them swim the channel. We'll go together. It will be warm and—"

"Mom . . ." Gracie's voice was just a whisper. "I'm not going to Chincoteague, and we both know it."

Gracie looked so small in the bed. She didn't look like a teenager, but just a little girl. A very sick little girl. But unlike when she was little, no amount of stories or cool cloths on her forehead would make her feel better.

Lexie noticed the corner of Gracie's old orange blanket sneaking out from beneath her pillow and for some reason, it made her tear up. Gracie had long since tucked the blanket into a drawer. She'd no longer needed its comfort . . . until now.

"Gracie, miracles happen." Lexie clung to that idea. For the last six months, she'd clung to that. The doctors talked about stage four, about treatments, finally about hospice, but still Lexie clung to the idea that a miracle was going to happen. That something would happen to save her Gracie. Her peacemaker. Her youngest.

"No miracle this time, Mom. And I'm sad that I'm not going to learn to drive, or graduate, but Mom, there are so many things . . ."

Gracie paused and drew a long but shallow breath. "I'm grateful . . ."

She drifted off.

Lee came in. Lexie didn't need to turn to know it was him. She knew his footsteps.

These last few weeks, as her life contracted and grew smaller, it took on a new rhythm that centered on Gracie. With her life so narrowly focused, Lexie had learned the sounds of the house in an entirely new way. Her two Cons had gradually traded in their heavy-footed steps for lighter, almost tiptoed ones. And Lee, his footsteps spoke of a hesitancy that he'd never had before.

It was good that she recognized his footsteps, because he said very little to her. Lexie felt as if he blamed her for Gracie's illness. She understood his anger—she was angry too. She was angry at the terrible disease that had her daughter in its sights. She was angry with a God who would let someone like Gracie suffer like this. Some days her anger was all that kept her going.

Under its fire, she could move from one task to the next.

But she wasn't angry with Lee, or her kids. She wasn't sure why he was angry with her. They should stand together and support each other. Instead, they were distant with each other and it felt as if, as Gracie's health continued its downward spiral, the distance between them widened.

Normally when Lee was out of sorts, Lexie did whatever she could to pull him from his funk. But this time, she didn't have the energy to stave off his mood. It was all she could do to keep herself together for Gracie's sake.

"Lexie, can I talk to you?" Lee beckoned her into the hall. It was as far as she would go. She'd stuck to Gracie's side for weeks and she wasn't budging. She stood at the door, where she could watch her sleeping daughter.

"You have to stop talking about miracles." Despite his hushed whisper, Lee's anger was palpable. "Gracie's made her peace. Our job now is to make it as easy on her—"

"Easy?" Lexie asked, her whisper strangled with her own anger, which suddenly had a target. "You want me to make it easy on my daughter— my barely sixteen-year-old daughter—to leave me? Hell no. I won't do it. I'm her mother. I'm here to protect her, even if that means protecting her from you and everyone else who says there's no hope. There's always hope."

And just like that, Lee's anger faded. Lexie had witnessed Lee's profound sadness in the past, but this was deeper. It was complete.

"Lex," he said sadly and moved as if to pull her into an embrace. Or maybe he reached for her to cling to her, like a drowning man grabbing for something to hold on to.

But Lexie couldn't prop Lee up. She could barely keep her own head above water. So she yanked herself back from his grasp. "I won't give up on her."

She went back into Gracie's room and shut the door on Lee. She watched her daughter sleep.

Gracie. Her baby. Her child.

Her heart.

The idea of losing her youngest was so abhorrent, it made her feel physically sick to her stomach.

She hadn't been close to God in a long time, but as she sat by Gracie's bed, she bargained with Him. If He let her daughter get better, she'd go back to church. She'd say a prayer of thanks every day.

As the days passed, her prayers became more frantic. She begged God to take her and let Gracie live. Anything. She'd do anything, make any deal, if only he'd save her daughter.

But God wasn't listening.

Gracie grew smaller and smaller in that bed. So small that even Chincoteague stories were too big. They didn't help. Instead, Gracie asked for a few of her favorite storybooks, but rarely could stay awake for something as short as *Where the Wild Things Are*.

So small, so tired, so fragile . . .

"I can't tell any more tonight," I said. I could smell that room. Even after so many years I knew that scent. Sam had talked about realizing he was in a hospital because of the smell. That's how Gracie's room had smelled at the end. Of medications and antiseptics. Of bodily functions she could no longer control.

It had smelled of despair. My despair, not Gracie's. Like her name, Grace had accepted what was coming long before I could.

"I sat by her bed for a long time and when even the shortest storybook was too long, I talked about going to see the ponies at Chincoteague when she was better."

We never went to Chincoteague.

I choked back my tears and rage at that thought.

I looked at Sam and tried not to plead as I asked, "Your one-thing?"

I knew my question sounded desperate. I needed to hear his one-thing, to think about Sam and something other than my daughter.

"I gave up," Sam announced.

Sam sat in the wheelchair, staring out the window at the rolling hills of Pittsburgh.

It wasn't that he took note of how picturesque the southwestern Pennsylvanian city was. He didn't. It was just something to stare at.

His mother had been in yesterday. She'd talked to him of family news and the small happenings in her life. He thought about responding. Even tried once. But it seemed to take more energy than he had.

It had been three months since he'd woken up. He'd stopped—stopped talking, stopped being angry and railing against the fates, stopped thinking. He'd stopped it all as completely as when he'd initially arrived at the hospital in a coma.

The physical therapist came in and manipulated his shattered leg.

Sam didn't participate or complain. He complacently accepted the pain as if it were a penance—as if it could somehow help assuage some of the guilt he felt.

It didn't work.

His mother came, day after day, and continued to talk to him. One day, she suddenly burst into tears and left.

He should have called out to her. Just one word would have heartened her, but he couldn't seem to manage even that.

When he was little, his mother's tears were enough to stop him in his tracks. She'd cried the time he'd gone out drinking with his friends and had been picked up by the local police. He'd never done it again.

Now, he just couldn't work up the energy to feel bad.

When she left, the room got quiet and he went back to staring.

Light to dark. Dark to light.

Someone bringing food.

Someone manipulating his leg.

He barely noted those variations.

He recalled a doctor coming in and talking about post-traumatic stress and using words like *elective mutism*.

Even that couldn't shake him from the listlessness.

Then sometime later—hours, days, he wasn't sure—he heard heavier footsteps come into the room.

He sensed someone standing behind him, but couldn't work up the energy to turn and see who.

"Come on, Sam. It's time to get up."

His surprise was the impetus he needed to turn. "Grid?"

"So, Romeo, you can talk. Told 'em that Samuel Adams Corner wasn't a quitter. I was right. Now, get up."

Sergeant Harrison Gridley was a friend. He'd been there the day . . .

Sam's momentary spurt of energy evaporated and he sank back into his seat, longing to just go back to staring and not thinking.

"So, that's it?" Grid was pissed. It didn't take any special abilities to hear it in his voice.

"You got nothing to say?"

Grid pulled a chair over and moved into Sam's line of sight.

"Listen, I know this isn't about your messed-up leg and other injuries. You're too tough to stop over that." He paused, as if Sam had answered. "I get it. It hurts. Ramsey, Smith, Johnson, Lyle, and Lennon. Their names are part of me. They always will be. I miss them, too, but you can't just stop because of it."

He stood, pushed back the chair, and got the walker that stood in the corner.

"Your PT guy said you should be walking. Hell, Sam, you should be talking and getting on with your life."

Grid reached down and threw the brakes on Sam's wheelchair. "Come on."

Sam couldn't make himself reach for the walker.

"That's it? You're going to just stop? All those guys who didn't get a choice, who aren't going home, who will never hug their moms or their girls again, and you're just going to give all that up willingly? I thought you were brave, Sam, but you're not. You're a coward."

He turned and walked toward the door. Then turned again. "You're dishonoring the boys— you're dishonoring every man who fought over there and will never have a chance to come home and live their life."

Grid left before Sam could try and find the words to tell him that he didn't understand. Grid was right—it wasn't Sam's leg; it was . . . everything. A huge weight had settled over him. Grid was wrong; Sam didn't have a choice. It wasn't the pain of his injuries, but the pain of those losses.

He sat in the wheelchair, staring at the walker. He wished he could go back to just staring out the window. He wished that Grid hadn't come and disturbed his peace.

No, peace wasn't the right word.

But he didn't have the energy to figure out what the word would be.

❦

"Inertia," Sam said.

I nodded. I got that. More than most people would.

"Every day Grid came to visit and pushed and prodded. He had the therapist show him what to do, and then he did it. Over and over. He twisted my leg. He pulled at it, stretching the damaged muscles. But more than that, he twisted me and pulled me from wherever it was I'd been hiding . . ."

Two weeks after Grid arrived, he sat across from Sam.

"Do you remember that night they served hot dogs and you started rhapsodizing about Smith Hot Dogs? They're a western Pennsylvania thing, and you went on and on about how no other hot dogs could compare?"

Despite himself, Sam was pulled into the memory. "Lyle said he was a hot dog expert because he'd competed in hot-dog-eating contests, and since he'd never heard of them, how good could they be?"

Grid nodded. "And you challenged him to a duel. The guys cheered and egged the two of you on."

"Lyle won and I threw up."

"But they cheered as you puked," Grid said with pride in his voice. Then his smile faded. "What would they think if they saw you now?"

Sam didn't answer. He was still in the middle of that memory.

"I've been here two weeks, Sam. You're talking now, and that's good. But it's not enough. You've got to get up. It's time. You've mourned them. Now it's time to honor them. Get up."

Sam remembered Lyle and their hot dog debate. Ramsey, a family man, had four girls. He used

81

to joke that being deployed was his only defense against all that estrogen.

Smith was a musician when he wasn't fighting in wars. Even now, Sam could hear the soft refrain of *Red River Valley*.

Johnson was an outdoorsman. He swore when he got home he was heading to Alaska. He longed for snow and ice. He was going to fish and lose himself in the wilderness there.

And Lennon, who was just one of the boys, even if she was a girl. She could spit, belch, and tell a tall tale along with the rest of them. But sometimes, there was a softness that crept around her rough edges. That little girl on their last trip. She'd held her as if she were the girl's mother.

Sam felt the weight of their loss. It pressed on him, driving him back into himself.

Grid seemed to sense it. "No you don't," he said, and punched Sam in the arm, not as hard as he could, but hard enough to remind Sam he could still feel.

"Get up, Sam." Grid's voice was fierce. "You know they all would be pissed if they could see you here, wallowing. Just get up. That first step is always the hardest."

Without a word, Sam reached down and fumbled with the brakes on the wheelchair.

He reached for the walker.

"Just one step, Sam. Once the first one's over,

the second will be easier, and then the third, then . . ."

Sam threw his weight forward and let momentum do the bulk of the work. He rose, unsteady.

"Just the first step," Grid whispered.

And Sam reached his right leg forward, and set it inches in front of the left.

It wasn't much of a step, but Grid was right; it was the hardest.

❧

"I'm sorry," I said.

"Me, too," Sam echoed.

That was all. Maybe it didn't seem like much to Jerry, who was nursing his beer at the end of the bar, probably listening to us again.

But I knew it was something big.

Something huge.

Chapter Eight

That week, things felt different. Somehow lighter. Sam's friend's words resonated with me. Sometimes you needed to take time to collect yourself.

The first step is the hardest.

I'd taken a year and wasn't sure I'd collected myself very much. I still felt . . . adrift. Lost.

Then I thought about it, and realized maybe I had taken a first step. I had friends now. Someplace to go every Monday. I felt as if I managed to reconnect with the kids.

I had the tapestry.

How had that very imperfect piece of cloth on my loom become so important? I wasn't sure, but it was.

I took Angus on a long walk on Tuesday. I owed him after last week's neglect. It was cool enough that I needed a jacket. I wore an old black-and-red flannel shirt that had been Conner's, once upon a time. He'd left it when he went to college, and I claimed it.

Even though it had been years and it had thinned after repeated washings, I swore it kept me warmer than my fleece jacket. And it reminded me of my son. The boy he was, and the man he'd become.

He was a cop.

How an accountant and an art teacher had produced a law enforcement officer boggled me, but we had and he was.

He'd been a good kid, and now he was a good man, keeping people safe in Erie. He believed in what he was doing. I envied him that. I was no longer sure what I believed in.

Angus bounded through the woods, barking wildly at everything and nothing.

"Come on, Gus," I hollered. We walked and I waited for inspiration to claim me. That's how it was when I walked. I'd think about my current project and I'd suddenly know what came next. Or I'd have a design for some pottery.

Now, I wanted to know what I should stitch into my tapestry next. What I should work on between my Monday excursions.

My life had settled into a rhythm. Mondays, then work until it was Monday again. I needed something to work on this week. Angus and I walked for hours that Tuesday morning waiting for direction for this week to come.

But nothing came.

With or without inspiration, it was time to go back. It really was cold.

It took me more than a minute to realize that it was October.

The summer had well and truly left.

"Gus."

There were leaves that had already surrendered to the inevitable and fallen. My Wellingtons crunched against them as I walked. Hickory nuts littered the path too. My boots crushed them into the soft earth. Some might sprout into seedlings next spring.

And now that I was noticing things, I noticed that the leaves that remained in the trees were red, gold, and orange. The few remaining evergreens provided a touch of green that would accent the dark brown limbs throughout the winter.

And then I knew. I absolutely knew with certainty what I needed to add next.

I was anxious to get back to the workshop.

I worked hard that week, but not with the same manic need as last. Telling Sam about Gracie had been some sort of hurdle, I realized, as I added a swatch of water and sand next to the horse and orange blanket that week. Then, I ringed the tableaux with fall flowers. I was starting to say good-bye to Gracie, my peacemaker. My heart. Finally. Years later I could say good-bye.

I had hoped and prayed for that miracle, but it never came. Gracie had died. It was a Sunday morning, still dark and quiet. The newspaper boy who tossed our daily paper onto the porch—I'd learned the distinct sound of that thud—still hadn't come by.

I was bone weary. I'd had Lee help me move one of the family room recliners into Gracie's room. My asking, "Could you help me move a recliner?" was the longest conversation we'd had in days. Ever since our miracle disagreement, we'd stopped talking altogether.

I spent most of my nights in Gracie's room in order to hear her whenever she needed me.

But that night, she'd asked me to hold her as she slept. I'd snuggled next to her in her bed for a very long time, until I was certain she was sleeping. Then I moved over to the recliner. She hadn't called. I'd woken up and realized that she'd finally had a peaceful night's sleep. Maybe she was better. Maybe I had my miracle.

I'd given her the morphine about midnight. It supplemented her pain patch. She'd slept quietly after that.

I remember thinking that maybe Gracie had turned some corner and would be better. I'd watched her from my recliner vantage point. Her expression was peaceful and I'd wondered what she'd dreamed about. Then

I realized, her chest wasn't rising or falling anymore.

Horror sank in. Sometime after midnight, as I slept, she'd quietly left.

Even all these years later, I felt the stab of pain again. I'd lost Gracie.

I think that's when I started losing myself as well.

Maybe I'd started when my father died.

But now, sitting in my studio, working on the tapestry, I finally started letting go of Gracie.

No, that was wrong. I could never let go of her. But I could let go of the pain of her loss and remember the joy and the grace of my youngest daughter.

That week I felt as if my baggage was lighter.

I bundled up before I walked to The Corner Bar on Monday. I walked slower than I normally did because I knew what part of my story I had to tell next. I didn't want to, but I knew it had to be the next one.

The bar seemed warm and inviting as I entered.

"Colder than a witch's tit," Jerry called jovially as I entered. " 'Course, I have no idea how cold that would be, but this is colder."

He laughed and took another sip of his beer.

Jerry was a sipper.

Over the last few weeks, as I started coming

back to life and began paying attention, I'd learned that he came to the bar for company more than to drink. It was as if I was suddenly noticing that the bar had more occupants than just Sam and me. It came as a surprise. I realized that I'd become a bit myopic, focusing on just a few things, not the world in its entirety. I was going to try to change that.

I waved at Joanie, the waitress, and as I passed Jerry, I asked, "Did you have a good weekend?"

"Sure did. Got every leaf on my lawn raked up. Of course, I came out this morning, and there was a whole new batch waiting for me to rake 'em."

"Leaves and laundry. You never entirely finish either," was my sage response.

Jerry laughed as Sam came toward me, my Killian's in its iced glass in his hand, and said the words that had become my permission to seek release. "One thing."

"My miracle never came. Gracie's miracle. It wasn't long after I lost her that I lost everyone else."

❧

"Hey, Mom," Connie said over the phone.

"Hi, honey. How's school?" Connie always swore she couldn't wait to get out of Erie. Lexie had never understood that. She loved Erie. She loved the entire northwestern Pennsylvania region. But true to her word, Connie had decided on OSU in neighboring Ohio. Conner had stayed closer. He was at Pitt, just a couple hours away in Pittsburgh.

Early morning calls had become Lexie's mainstay.

She sipped her coffee and listened as Connie talked about her classes and friends. Connie asked about school and Lexie tried to come up with happy anecdotes, but for the first time in her teaching career, her students didn't excite her. Teaching had become a chore. She dreaded getting up and going to school each morning.

"It's great, honey," she said with horribly false enthusiasm. "We're getting ready for an art show."

"You know, Mom, you should show some of your stuff. That dish you made me for my keys is right by the door. Everyone comments on it."

Lexie hadn't been working on her pottery in a long time. Not since—

She shut off the thought, but couldn't shut off the flash of pain. "Well, I've got to run, sweetie."

"I talked to Dork-Boy yesterday." She didn't need to ask who Connie meant—the entire family was well aware of her nickname for her twin. "He'll call tonight."

"Great. But you don't have to make him call."

"I didn't make him, Mom. I just prodded a little." She laughed and Lexie forced herself to try to echo it. She hoped that Connie didn't notice that it didn't ring true.

Lee walked into the room and mouthed the words, *Tell her I said hi.*

"Your dad says hi."

"Hi back at him. Gotta run."

Connie clicked off. "She said hi as well."

Lee poured himself some coffee and picked up the paper.

This was their new routine. He came downstairs each day just as Lexie was ready to leave for school. He came home as she was going up to bed. After Gracie died, something in their marriage had died as well. Lexie wasn't sure what it was, but she felt its absence.

On the off chance tonight would be different, she asked, "Will you be home for dinner?"

"No."

She wasn't sure why, but suddenly his response pissed her off. She hadn't cared enough about anything to be pissed off in a long time. The rush of anger felt good.

"Maybe it's time we admit this marriage is over," she said, without thinking. She hadn't realized that's what she'd been thinking.

Lee took a sip of his coffee and met her gaze.

She waited for him to express some emotion. Anger. Pain. Or maybe he'd laugh and tell her don't be silly. They'd gone through bad periods before—times when they lost each other for a moment. But then the moment passed and they always came back to themselves.

There was no anger, no pain, no laughing at the idea of them not being together—not being Lexie and Lee.

Since that first day on the quad when he'd joked that if they married they'd have the same initials, they'd been Lexie-and-Lee. Their names fitting together as well as they did.

Good times and bad. They'd stuck.

She remembered his wedding vows. Talking about chemical reactions in reference to that first day on the quad.

When it came to her vows, she'd told him, "I didn't want them to use the words 'until death do us part,' because it won't. I promise that I will love you forever."

She looked at him now and their wedding day felt too far away to count, and that promise felt burdensome.

"Lee?" she prodded, needing him to say something. "Say something."

She needed him to be strong this once. She needed him to pull her into his arms and tell her everything would be okay . . . even if it was a lie.

But he didn't move. He nodded. "Maybe it is time to admit our marriage has been over since—" He cut himself off.

Neither of them was ready to voice when their marriage had died. But Lexie knew the exact moment. The moment that she woke up to discover her daughter would never wake up again.

She should be crying. She should be mourning the end of her marriage, but she didn't have room to mourn for anything other than Gracie. She thought about her mom's practicality when her father died.

Practicality to mask the pain.

She'd never given her mother enough credit. "Do you want to move out, or want me to?"

"I will," he said conversationally, as if they were simply discussing dinner plans. "Paul left his wife a few months ago. I can crash with him. I'll see to it this weekend."

And that was that. The man Lexie had been married to since she was twenty—for half of her life—was moving out.

They were calling it quits.

It was as if after Gracie died and the twins had left for their respective colleges, they had nothing left to bind them. Nothing left that they shared.

Lexie tried to think of something to cling to, some argument to mount, but she came up with nothing. She couldn't think of any earthly reason they should stay together. The only thing they shared anymore was a bed, and it was king-size, so they didn't even bump into each other.

There was nothing left.

"Well, all right then."

She let Bernie outside and left for school.

She walked out of the house and turned her back on half of her life.

☙

"Lexie, you did the best you could." Sam's words were offered as my absolution, but I knew he was wrong.

"No. No, I didn't. I could have fought. I could have tried. But it was easier to walk away. Nothing had been right since Gracie died. We'd become strangers. Lee had changed when she died. I'm sure I did, too. We limped along the year after we lost Gracie, while the twins were home, but when they left, there was no reason to put on any pretenses. It was over.

"And that's how you lost your husband?" Sam, who'd listened to all my stories—all my one-things—without judgment or comment, looked disappointed.

No, not disappointed. He looked mad.

When I didn't say anything, he pushed more. "You just gave up?"

Words I could say—maybe should say—tumbled over each other in my mind. That he thought he knew me well enough from just a few months of Monday one-things, that he could judge me and make assumptions . . . Well, it pissed me off. The anger I felt now echoed the anger I'd felt

94

that morning when Lee and I called it quits.

I pushed back my unfinished beer, grabbed my coat, and turned and walked out of the bar without saying anything.

I stomped down the road.

It wasn't long until he caught up with me. "Lex, wait."

"Fuck you, Sam," I shouted without turning around.

I had never used that word. Never.

I'd never even thought it.

Oh, I'd heard it. I was a teacher, so I was familiar with the sound of it. But it wasn't part of my personal lexicon.

Sam grabbed my arm and I tried to pull away, but he held tight and spun me. "I'm sorry."

"That wasn't how I lost him. Lee and I divorced . . ."

I hadn't planned to say more, even before Sam pissed me off. But the story came tumbling out.

❧

The twins graduated from college. Thankfully their ceremonies weren't the same weekend. Lexie was also thankful that she and Lee figured out how to coexist with the kids.

Their divorce hadn't just been amicable. It had been emotionless. Painless.

They'd both simply had enough and walked away.

It was as if they'd used up all their pain at Gracie's funeral and didn't have any left to mourn the death of their marriage.

Lexie had heard that losing a child was the worst kind of pain and she didn't doubt it. She felt as if someone had cut off a limb and she was suffering from phantom pains, thinking her arm was still there, even when it was long gone.

Some mornings, she woke up and forgot. Forgot that Lee had moved out. Forgot that her two Cons were away at college. Forgot that Gracie was dead.

The forgetting only lasted a few moments, but when she remembered, the pain hit her anew and she almost buckled under the weight of it.

Last weekend, at Connie's graduation, they'd sat as if they were a family. Lexie, Conner, then Lee. This week, the same thing, except it was Connie sitting in between them and Conner graduating.

As they sat in the huge theater the school had rented for its graduation, Lexie realized the seat next to hers was empty. For a moment—just the smallest of moments—she closed her eyes and pretended Gracie was there, sitting next to them at Conner's graduation. She reached over and placed her hand on the armrest that separated the seats, but instead of Gracie's hand, she just felt wood.

Gracie should have been sitting there, watching her brother graduate and talking about her own graduation the next year.

And even after years, the pain and anger hit her again.

Lee looked over Connie's shoulders and mouthed the word, "Gracie?"

Lexie nodded and felt the tears welling in her eyes.

Connie looked over and took her hand. "Mom, you don't have to cry. Dork-Boy got a job. He won't be moving in with you or dad and sponging off you. And to be honest, if the whole work thing doesn't work for him, I told him he could come live in my basement."

She laughed and allowed Connie to think that's what it was. It was easier that way.

They sat through the graduation.

Lexie had sat through them in the past for friends, but she'd never found much to recommend graduation ceremonies. Pompous guest speakers who went on and on about the future the graduates had in front of them, when all the graduates wanted to do was revel in the here and now—in the fact they'd accomplished this goal and had earned their diplomas.

Two hours of listening to endless names of people she didn't know in order to enjoy that one moment that belonged to her . . . to her friend or her child.

They called Conner's name and handed her son his diploma.

Lexie looked at Lee again, and smiled. He smiled back and she knew he understood what she was saying without words. *Congratulations.* They might have screwed up many things, but they'd done this right. They'd parented these two children into the start of successful adulthoods.

Then, just like that, it was done. The ceremony ended and Lexie reveled in the knowledge that somehow, despite everything, they'd managed to raise two amazing people. There would always be a hole in their lives where Gracie would live, but still, they'd managed it.

They were connected.

"Excuse me," Lexie said to a passing parent. "Would you take a picture of the four of us?"

"Sure."

"Camera karma?" Lee asked, laughing.

She nodded.

The father taking the picture motioned the four of them closer, and asked, "Camera karma?"

They'd started the family tradition on a trip to Disney World. Every time they'd offered to take a picture for another family, someone would turn up at just the right time and do the same for them.

Lee put his arm around Lexie and explained to the man, "You take a picture for me, and it's good camera karma. I'll offer to take one of your family . . . karma."

The man laughed, which made them laugh as well.

That moment was when their impromptu photographer snapped the picture. He held the camera out to Lexie and she looked at that moment captured in time. The four of them laughing. Happy.

Connie's shoulder-length blond hair fanning out, and Conner's hair covered by the cap he still wore. The twins sandwiched her and Lee, who had his arm around her, as he'd done in countless pictures when they were still married.

They might have lost their way and divorced, but they would always be tied by their twins.

Just as they'd always be tied by the child they'd lost.

As if he were thinking the same thing, Lee leaned over and peered at the picture, his hand slipping with a comforting familiarity around Lexie's waist.

She still felt a distant, familiar spark.

⟋⟍

"I hadn't lost him then; I'd just misplaced him for a bit," I explained to Sam.

"And after your son's graduation, you started seeing him again?"

"Well, not just then. It was a start, that touch. But it—Lee and I and what we had— we didn't find our way back fast or sudden."

"What—"

"No more tonight, Sam. I . . ." I paused, wanting to explain. "This thing on Mondays—whatever it is—it means something to me. It's cathartic. But to say it all at once . . ." I just shook my head.

He nodded. "And about earlier, I'm sorry. It's just that you don't strike me as the type who gives up. You didn't with Grace. You fought. And I admired that because I did give up. If it hadn't been for Grid . . ." He shrugged. "If it hadn't been for him, I might not have been able to start again."

✆

"You are not my mother. You're not my commander. Get the hell out." Grid moved toward him. "Get the hell away from me."

"Tut, tut, tut. Do you kiss your mother with that mouth? Kiss any women with that mouth? Probably not, because at the rate you're moving, you couldn't catch a woman to save your sorry ass. And you and I both know, with a face like that, you've got to do the catching, because no woman's going to come to you on her own."

"Grid . . ." Sam left the threat hanging because, truth was, he couldn't think of a threat he hadn't tried on Grid.

His friend had relocated to Pittsburgh and found an apartment near the rehab center. Sam had protested, saying Grid should go home, but Grid assured him that the only home he'd ever had was with his friends in the service, so Pittsburgh was as good a place as any. He got a job at a local bar working evenings so that he could spend his days torturing Sam.

"I'm tired," Sam said.

"Me too. Tired of all your pussy-boy whining. Now, get up and get your ass on the bars."

Sam flipped him the bird.

Grid reached down, hoisted Sam up, and dragged him with very little care or gentleness to the bars. "Walk."

"Mr. Gridley," the therapist hollered.

Sam could have told her it was useless. Just as he'd known himself it was useless. "Bite me, Grid."

"Listen, there were guys who didn't get to come home. If you won't do it for yourself, then do it for them. You owe them, Sam."

Sam swung at Grid, who neatly ducked out of the way, and Sam found himself sitting on the floor.

"Great. Get mad. I don't care. Just get your ass up and walk the bar. You get out of here, and maybe I'll leave you alone."

"Promise?"

Grid wouldn't let the therapist help him up, nor would he offer a hand himself. He waited and watched until Sam clawed his way back up to the bars, then slowly walked to the other end.

"I would have given up if it wasn't for Grid. I would have just sat back and stopped. But he pushed me. The therapists yelled about insurance issues and tried to keep him away. He didn't listen to them any more than he listened to me. He just kept hammering away at me. He wouldn't let me quit. I didn't imagine you giving up and the thought of it pissed me off."

I snorted. "You think you know me from whatever this is, but Sam, you don't know me at all yet."

"But you'll tell me?"

I wanted to say no. I wanted to let him live with his illusion of me being strong, just like Gracie had. But I knew I'd come too far to lie to him now, either by saying the words or by omitting them.

Lies of omission were still lies.

"I'll tell you. But I'm not sure you'll like it."

Chapter Nine

"Lexie, it's your mother," Mom announced over the phone late the next afternoon. She'd always started conversations that way, as if I wouldn't know who she was unless she told me. "I'm coming out for dinner."

"Mom, today's not a good day for me. I'm working on this project—" I'd been stitching a graduation cap into the tapestry. I'd worked on it all day today.

"Lexie, you and I both know that no day is a good day for you anymore. There haven't been any good days in a long, long time."

That was true a few months ago, but not anymore.

Mondays were good days.

It was as if talking to Sam brightened . . . well, everything. I felt the need to work again. I felt . . . I searched for a word. More alive.

I'd tried therapy, but I'd just ended up sitting across from some bottle-redheaded woman, staring at her and trying not to think about how much money I'd wasted in order to sit and stare at her.

But at The Corner Bar, for the price of a bottle of Killian's, I'd found my couch.

"Mom—"

"Don't cook. We're going out." She hung up.

"Great," I said to Angus. "Looks like I'm going out on a Tuesday."

I glanced in the mirror. Then did a double take. I looked . . . well, haphazard. As if I'd taken a shower and thrown on the first clean clothes I'd found, then pulled my wet hair back in a ponytail.

I probably looked that way because that's exactly what I'd done. My mother wouldn't believe I was okay if I didn't look the part. Marion Jones Morrow was a firm believer in putting on a social-face. "Looks like I'd better do some spit and polishing first."

Angus barked.

"Everyone's a critic," I muttered.

By the time my mother arrived, I had on a pair of jeans that had no holes and a shirt that Conner hadn't outgrown or Lee hadn't passed on to me.

I'd brushed my hair and even put on some eyeliner.

"Well, you look spiffy," my mother said as I opened the door for her. "For you," she added.

Mom still lived with the hope that someday I'd clean up properly and be wearing clothes I could introduce her to by name. I hated to shatter that hope, so I simply said, "Come on in, Mother."

She shook her head and remained firmly on the porch. "No. We're going out. I'm dragging you away from here, at least for a little while."

Angus hadn't even bothered getting up from his seat on the couch. I left him there, grabbed my keys and wallet and stuffed them in my pocket, then flipped the lock on the knob and shut the door. "So, where do you want to go?"

"To your bar. I assume they have food?"

I didn't want to take her to the bar. Maybe it was selfish, but I didn't want to share it. It was my place. "Maybe we could go into a restaurant in Union City or even Waterford. There's a restaurant at the old Eagle Hotel. It's supposed to be fantastic." The cottage sat about midway between both towns.

"Or we could go to your bar. I drove by it coming in. Come on, I'll drive."

My mother was a force of nature. At one time I'd stood against the Marion gale force winds, but though I felt better and stronger, I wasn't up to fighting against her yet. So we drove to The Corner Bar.

Sam was behind the bar. Jerry was in his normal seat.

I knew they were here every Monday night, but I'd never thought about other days or nights.

They both did a double take.

"My mom," I explained. "Marion Jones Morrow, this is Jerry—sorry, I don't know your last name."

He raked his fingers through his thinning hair—wisps, really—and stood. "Smith. Jerry Smith." He extended his hand.

My mother was all grace and manners as she shook Jerry's hand. "Mr. Smith. It's a pleasure."

"And this is my friend, Sam. Sam Corner." I remembered the first time I'd brought Lee home to meet my parents. His reception had been somewhere above frostbite, but just barely. But as I introduced Sam as my friend, my mother smiled at him. "Mr. Corner."

"Ma'am," he said with a courtly nod.

"We're here for dinner," she announced.

"We have great burgers and I think there's some chili still in the back."

It was kind of Sam to offer that much because I'd never eaten food here and wouldn't have known what my options were.

"Chili, please," I said.

"Me, too," Mom said and led me to a booth.

"So this is where you come on Mondays," she mused as she took in the bar.

I tried to see it as if I were seeing it for the first time. There were signs for various beers on the wall, some framed pictures and . . .

Sam set a glass down in front of me. It wasn't Killian's. It was a darker, richer color. Brown, almost black. And the foamy head on the beer was a layer unto itself and showed no signs of dissipating. I knew what it was without asking, but I wasn't sure how or why.

"I got a keg," Sam announced, answering the how, but not the why.

"Pardon?" I asked stupidly.

"I was going to surprise you next week. I have a keg of Guinness. Jerry said he'd switch over to it, and I've got a sign coming in, so hopefully we'll have a few regulars try it, too. I waited for you to tap it."

"You got a keg," I repeated.

Sam looked embarrassed as he nodded. "I thought I'd see if we could build a following. Might be good marketing. I don't think any other bar around here carries it on tap. And according to the experts, draught is the only way to drink it."

He shot my mom a charming smile. "It's not like other beers, I've been told. And when I bought the keg, my dealer told me there's an art to pouring a pint right. Thank goodness for YouTube. They had more than a hundred videos on how to do it. It's a two-part method of pouring a pint of Guinness." He nodded at my glass. "I did okay for a first attempt. But hey, if it takes off, I'll have it down to a science

107

soon. It's good business," he said again.

But we both knew it wasn't business. It was a gift.

I took his hand and squeezed it. "Thanks."

He smiled and we just stayed that way for a minute. Me smiling my thanks, holding his hand. Him smiling back at me.

My mom cleared her throat.

"Sorry. Ma'am, what can I get you to drink?"

"I'll have what she's having."

So there I was. At Sam's on a Tuesday with a pint of Guinness and my mom.

Sam didn't ask me one-thing.

I didn't offer one.

And yet, there'd been a moment. Just one small thing. And I'd learned that maybe that's what life was all about, one thing after another. One small moment. Good or bad.

This one was good. A very good moment.

My mother and I ate in companionable silence. I thought she'd grill me, or tell me how worried she was about me, but she simply ate.

"Mom?"

She looked up, still silent.

"Connie came out a few weeks ago. I told her about the day after dad died, when we went for a walk on the peninsula."

She smiled, as if the memory was a happy one for her as well. "I remember."

"I don't know if I ever told you how much that day meant to me. Every time I took Bernie for a walk, or snuggled with him, I thought of you."

"Some people might not see being compared to a dog as a compliment, but I understand what you're saying, and I do take it as such. Thank you."

"I never said it, but thank you, too."

"For a trip to the pound?"

"No, for letting me think that Dad was perfect. I think that day on the beach was the day I realized how much you loved me. Love me."

My mother blinked rapidly and I was struck with the thought that Marion Jones Morrow might be on the verge of tears.

"I know I've never been a demonstrative mother. I wasn't raised that way. My parents, your grandparents, weren't like that. I never learned how to be . . ." She hesitated, searching for a word. "Cuddly." She threw my own long-ago word back at me, but she smiled as if to say it was okay.

"But Lexie, I have loved you since the moment you were born. I would do anything for you. I let you believe your father was perfect because you needed someone more effusive than I could be."

I reached across the table and took her hand.

"I know that. That kind of unconditional love is precious. Thank you."

She squeezed my hand, then let go and took a sip of her Guinness. "This isn't what I imagined a Guinness would taste like."

"Do you like it?"

"Yes, very much."

Chapter Ten

I went back to The Corner Bar the following Monday.

I wasn't sure if the bar would feel different, now that I'd come with someone else on a day that wasn't a Monday. I worried that like a fairy-tale character, I'd somehow broken the magic by pressing for more.

I walked through the doorway that Monday evening and stood a moment. Maybe a third of the tables had people at them. The signs for various beers still twinkled merrily. Jerry sat on his regular barstool, and Sam turned from a drink he was making and smiled at me.

A wave of relief swept through me. The bar was still the same. My Monday magic was still in place.

Relief spread through my body as Sam slid me a pint of the Guinness. It made me smile.

I took a long sip of the thick, frothy head. "Now, that's a beer."

"One thing," he said, sounding as cheerful as I felt.

"The kids had graduated and were both working adults. Lee and I were divorced. I still wasn't doing any of my own pottery, or anything else that could be remotely labeled artistic. But I was dating a very nice man named Jensen and I was happy. Not one of those bone-deep happinesses, but a quiet, not-in-pain sort. It was quite a lovely respite."

"Degrees of happiness?" Sam asked.

I nodded.

⁂

Lexie hummed as she got ready for her date with Jensen. He was a nice man. A banker. Not a teller, but rather someone who sat at a desk and gave out loans and investment advice. He liked to talk about work. It wasn't exactly scintillating conversation. She frequently zoned out as he droned on and on, but she found the sound of his voice soothing. She liked that what he did excited him, even if the idea of working with numbers and money all day gave her the willies and occasionally reminded her of Lee.

The doorbell rang and she hurried down the stairs.

"Jens—" was as far as she got, because it wasn't him. It was Lee.

"You look nice," he said.

She glanced down at her khaki-colored pants and simple black shirt. She'd added a scarf and thought it gave her a jaunty, carefree look, but she wasn't sure she liked that Lee had noticed. They were divorced. He shouldn't notice how she was dressed. But instead of saying that, or

112

even mentioning she'd been thinking about him, she simply said, "Uh, thanks."

"You're going out?"

She nodded.

"Then I won't keep you. I'm going to Connie's on Saturday. Just for the day. I thought maybe you'd like to come along."

"With you?" Drive to Cleveland with her ex? That didn't sound wise, despite the momentary spurt of interest.

He nodded.

"To see Connie?"

He nodded again.

"You never asked me when she was in college and you were going to visit."

"I'm asking now," he said simply.

Lexie had been feeling happy a few moments ago as she got ready for her date with Jensen, but as she thought about spending a day with Lee, she felt beyond mildly happy. She felt practically giddy.

Giddy with glee.

It had been a long time since she'd felt that way.

"Yes." I looked at Sam. "I told him yes. And for the first time in a very long time, I didn't just feel happy. Happy can be a flat, sort of even, word. It's a go-with-the-flow and fill-in-the-cracks word. I'm not sad or mad, so I must be happy. But standing there, at my door, dressed for a date with another man, a nice man, talking about spending a day in the car with my ex-husband, I felt glee. And glee is as different from happy as sad is from despair."

"Degrees of happy," he repeated. This time it was a statement, not a question.

"Yes."

I didn't want him to ask what happened next. I didn't want to remember that now. I wanted to bask in the warm glow of that long-ago glee. So, I asked, "One thing?"

"Through no fault of my own, I healed."

✺

"Well, I'm leaving," Grid said one day, out of the blue.

Sam had been out of rehab for six months. Though he still used a cane, he felt as if he was walking well. His mother had been after him to move back home with her. She tried to sound convincing when she told him that she was lonely since his father died. But he knew she was dating a new guy, and figured the last thing she needed was a grown son hanging around.

He knew she loved him, but right now, her love felt suffocating. She would have waited on him hand and foot, and wouldn't understand he didn't need that. He couldn't deal with it. Grid, on the other hand, made it a point of not waiting on him. If he wanted a drink, then he damned well better haul himself off the couch and get it.

Even when Grid pissed him off, Sam knew that his friend understood his need to be self-sufficient.

So he'd gently told his mother no and stayed in town at an apartment he rented with Grid. A run-down, two-bedroom in Oakland. Grid had made sure he'd rented something with stairs—which wasn't hard since Oakland felt as if it were one giant hill. He claimed the extra steps were part of Sam's PT.

"Hot date?" Sam asked. Grid had a way with women. He genuinely liked them. Oh, he didn't stick with one for any length of time, but he didn't use them. He liked them, and they liked him in return.

"No, I've got a job offer. A security firm in California. I'm taking it. Who knows, maybe some hot starlet's going to meet me and fall under my spell."

The star part was meant to be humor, and somehow Sam managed to laugh, but it was hard because he knew the job part wasn't a joke. He counted on Grid. When everyone else pussyfooted around him, Grid just called things as he saw them and didn't take any guff.

Sam realized how much he was going to miss him. "Oh. That's great, Grid."

"The bar's going to need a new bartender with me gone. Chuck said come on down and interview. And by interview, he means you've got the job."

Sam shook his head. "I'm not sure I can stand eight hours a day."

"I mentioned that you were a bit gimpy, though he's met you, so he knows. He said you could have the afternoon shift; it's slower then. And he doesn't have a problem with you sitting down on the job."

Sam was better, but he wasn't sure he was ready to be out in the real world on a daily basis. "I—"

"Listen, I kicked your ass before, don't make me do it again. It's a job. It's some cash in your pocket and it will get you out with people. You don't realize it, but you need people."

"Grid, you are a pain in the ass." When Grid had first come to town Sam had said those words, or something similar, practically every day. But now, he said it with no anger or frustration, but rather with gratefulness. Without Grid, he might still be in that rehab hospital staring out a window.

"A pain in the ass who is generally right. I know, I know; it's a curse. I try not to flaunt my rightness, but hey, it's there. Like an elephant in the room. You can't help but notice that I'm right so often."

"When's your flight?" Sam asked, with a grin, which he knew had been Grid's intent.

"Tomorrow morning. But tonight, we're going down to the bar and I'm going to introduce you around."

"Go to hell," he said, without much heat.

"Buddy, we were already there and, through no fault of our own, we made it back. It's time we both find whatever measure of happiness we can."

❦

"Thanks to Grid, I healed. I worked in the bar. I made friends. I rebuilt my life. Later, I bought this place and met you." He took my hand.

"I'm glad," was all I said in response. Just two small words, but they conveyed so much.

And that was that. We both had ended the night's one-things on a happy note.

They weren't winning-the-lottery, giant sort of notes, but rather quiet, gleeful, leaving a very dark place and finding out there was a life waiting for you. It might not be the life you thought you were going to have, but it could be good . . .

In my book, that made for a very good Monday.

Chapter Eleven

I was in the workshop on Wednesday, staring at the loom and my project. I was sure a seasoned weaver would find a hundred flaws in the project.

I got up and walked to a picture on the barn wall. It was of an Amish quilt. I'd found it at a craft show and loved it. There was a quote in calligraphy on the matting. "Every quilt has an intentional flaw because the only thing that's perfect is God."

I loved that sentiment.

The picture had hung in my classroom, back when I was teaching.

I'd found my worst students were those in the honors program. They were accustomed to studying and working their way to As. They thought success in a class meant perfection. With my students' art projects, I didn't grade so much on the perfection or success of a project, but rather on the passion in the attempt.

I walked back to the tapestry and ran my fingers over the pictures. No, it wasn't perfect, but I'd poured my heart into the attempt.

I sat back on the stool and waited for

inspiration to strike, to tell me what to work on next. Angus leapt from the couch and ran to the door, barking manically.

As he paused for a breath, I heard it, too—a car.

It was rare that anyone visited me at the cottage. Rarer still that someone visited uninvited and unannounced.

I opened the door and a cold wind bit into me. My workshop was cool so I was dressed in jeans and a sweatshirt, but they did nothing to stop the wind from blowing right through me.

A beat-up gold truck was sitting in front of the house. Angus was barking at the driver's side door. His size intimidated most people, but obviously not this driver, because the door opened and Sam Corner got out.

"Sam?" I called as I hurried over. "Is something wrong?"

He patted Angus's head and before my eyes, Angus turned into a pussycat. He rubbed his giant head against Sam's thigh, indicating more head rubbing was required.

Sam smiled up at me as he obliged Angus and continued petting him. "No. Nothing's wrong. I just thought . . ."

"Yes?"

"I love our Mondays. They're helping me, and I think they're helping you. But I wanted to see you somewhere that wasn't a Monday and wasn't at the bar. Don't get me wrong, I want to hear the rest of your story and tell you the rest of mine, but that's our pasts. I wanted a chance to do something in the here and now. Something that wasn't about what happened before to you or me. So I thought maybe I could convince you to have a picnic with me."

He reached in the bed of the truck and pulled out a basket. An actual picnic basket.

"It's nothing special, just some sandwiches I threw together, but if you can take a break . . ." He let the sentence hang there, not quite a question.

"Sure." I wasn't sure that sounded enthusiastic enough. "I mean, yes. I'd like that. I'd like that a lot."

"Great."

A huge gust of wind roared through the hollow where the cottage sat.

"Maybe today's not the best day for a picnic. I mean, it's Halloween next week. It's way too late in the season for a picnic," Sam said.

"We could picnic in the cottage," I offered. I could have suggested the workshop, but I hadn't covered the tapestry and I wasn't ready to share that yet. Not even with Sam.

"You're sure you don't mind?"

"Of course not. It would be great."

I led him into the small cottage. When Lee and I had built it, we'd planned on it being mainly a summer retreat. There was this one great-room, with the kitchen/dining area at one end and the living area at the other. There was no television. We were out far enough that there was no cable, and reception for satellite was horrible because of all the trees. But even if it had been readily available, we wouldn't have put a television in. We wanted our time out here to be about each other, to be about the kids and the family.

And even now that I'd admitted I lived here, that it wasn't simply a summer cottage, I hadn't had a television installed because I hadn't felt the lack. I liked the quiet. When I wanted some noise, I had an iPod. That was enough.

I wondered what Sam thought as he looked around my home.

There were plates with the kids' handprints on the far wall. A Dale Gallon print of Strong Vincent that I'd bought for Lee, who was a huge Civil War buff.

"Come on in and make yourself at home," I offered, thankful that I'd already laid out a fire. It only took a quick kiss of a match to start it.

"Let me clear off the coffee table. I mean, I could put a blanket on the floor, but odds are Angus would consider food set out on the floor an invitation and—"

"The coffee table's fine, Lexie."

I picked up the bowl filled with pinecones that I used as a centerpiece.

"That's beautiful," Sam said.

I felt my cheeks warm. "I made it."

"I still have the jar you made me. I keep it on my counter for change." He took the bowl from me and examined it. "You have a gift. It must be amazing to make something tangible on a daily basis. Something solid. Something that will last. I've always thought art was a sort of immortality."

I felt obliged to explain, or maybe apologize for my lack of work. "I don't do much pottery anymore. I mean, I have a wheel and kiln, but I've been working on a non-pottery project."

"Oh, what?"

The tapestry felt like a Monday thing. Like a one-thing. And today wasn't about that, so I said, "I'll tell you about it sometime."

Sam must have understood, because he didn't press. "So, let's talk about something easy. Something people on first dates talk about."

I thought a moment, then threw out a conversational starter. "Movies? Books?"

"Movies," he said. "Your all-time favorite?"

*Star Trek.**

He started laughing. "I figured you'd say something all weepy and girly. *Titanic*, maybe?"

"I am so not a chick-flick sort of girl. Personally, I liked Cameron's *Avatar* a lot more than *Titanic*. I'm all about action. Sci-fi. I've been a *Star Trek* fan for years and love the way J. J. Abrams has reimagined the series. And let's not even start on my major crush on Joss Whedon and his shows. *Dr. Horrible* was . . ."

We talked about movies and books. We talked about the weather and local politics. We talked. We ate. We laughed.

There were no painful revelations. It was a Wednesday, not a Monday. And it turns out that Wednesdays were a day for the here and now. We were just two people enjoying each other's company.

Two hours later, Sam finally rose. "I really need to get going."

I stood as well and started packing things in his picnic basket.

"Lex?" he asked softly.

I looked up. "Yes?"

"Could we do this again? Maybe next time we could go out to a movie, or something like a real date."

I nodded. "I'd like that. I'd like that a lot."

He took the basket in one hand and my

hand in his other one as I walked him out to his truck. Angus danced around us, having decided that Sam was his new best friend.

When we reached the truck, he put the basket in the back, then turned to me. "I had a very nice time. Thanks."

"Me too. And thank you."

We stood for a moment. I knew what Sam was going to do before he did it, and I welcomed it.

He leaned down and gently kissed me.

His lips planted against mine for just a breath's length. My lips accepted the touch. I didn't deepen the kiss, nor did I pull away. It was an introductory kiss, and I simply accepted it as the gift it was.

Wednesdays were for the here and now, and here and now, this kiss was perfect.

Sam pulled back. "I'll see you Monday, and then maybe we can make plans for another day next week? Weekends will always be out for me—at least until I hire another bartender—but I can make other days work."

"Weekdays are fine with me. We'll make plans on Monday," I agreed.

"We're having a Halloween party at the bar on Saturday. Maybe you'd come?"

If I hadn't gone to the bar on a non-Monday with my mother, I might have said no. But I had, and it hadn't changed the magic of

Mondays, so I didn't feel any trepidation as I nodded. "I'd like that."

"Costumes are mandatory," he said. He hesitated for a moment, and I thought he might kiss me again, but instead, he got in the truck.

I held on to Angus as Sam backed up to the turnaround, then drove up the hill toward the road.

Angus licked my hand, as if to let me know it was okay to let go.

I did.

I let go of Angus, and not for the first time, I felt as if I might be ready to let go of the past and find a future.

Thanks to Sam.

Chapter Twelve

I agonized over a costume for Saturday night's Halloween party.

My first inclination was to go as a ghost. It was a simple, straightforward, traditional costume. But as I fingered an old sheet, I decided against it. A ghost was something that lurked in the shadows. I felt as if that's where I'd been living the last year—in the shadows—and I was done with that.

Maybe I'd go as an artist. But it had to be someone everyone would recognize. There were no world-renowned potters that had that kind of instant recognition. So, any artist.

Van Gogh? I could wrap a towel around my ear and . . .

No, I decided quickly. He'd killed himself.

I wanted to go as something happy. Upbeat. That's how I was feeling. My picnic with Sam was a lot of the reason why. But it was more than that. Our one-things were helping. I felt closer to the kids. And I felt I was connecting with my mother for the first time in a long time. Maybe the first time, period. We'd built a new relationship after my father's passing and we'd been closer, but we'd never really connected until recently.

So no depressed, suicidal artists for me.

And suddenly I knew what I wanted to be.

It required a trip to Erie to pick up an important part of the costume, but as I surveyed my image in the car mirror before I went into Sam's party, I felt like I'd made the right choice.

I hurried into the bar and spotted Sam immediately. He was dressed in a tweed jacket, with a pair of wire-rimmed glasses and an unlit pipe in his mouth. "Psychiatrist?" I asked. He nodded and I laughed. "I get it. Bartenders and psychiatrists are just different sides of the same coin."

"Well, you're the only who's got it. Jerry wanted to know if I was Sherlock Holmes." He sounded disgruntled.

"Jerry," I scolded. "He couldn't be Sherlock . . . no deerstalker hat." I studied our end-of-the-bar friend and laughed. He was wearing a postal worker outfit. *"Cheers?"* I asked.

"Cliff Clavin at your service, ma'am."

I laughed. "Perfect, Jerry."

"So, what are you?" Sam asked.

I took off my jacket, untied my striped scarf, and let my wild, teased hair loose. Then I carefully put my glasses on and took the unglazed clay pot out of my bag.

"Harry Potter?" Jerry asked.

"No, she's a Hairy *Potter*. H-A-I-R-Y." Jerry looked confused so Sam explained. "She does pottery. She's a potter."

"But there are no universal potters I could think of, so I went for—"

"A hairy potter," Jerry finished. "That's a good one."

"Well, it's only good if people know I made pottery. Otherwise, it requires an explanation."

"Still, it's creative," Jerry said.

Sam handed me a Guinness and said, "Go mingle. It's a party."

I did mingle. I explained my costume and I met people. Some I recognized, some who must have frequented the bar on other nights I didn't.

I spent almost an hour talking to Mike and Emma. They had a small farm out my way. They raised llamas and kids. "Saturday nights are our night out," Emma said. "We have a neighbor girl who comes to stay with the kids."

"How many?"

"Four," she said. "We thought we were done after our third, but seems God had other ideas."

Lee and I had thought we were done after the twins. Gracie was a surprise baby.

I remembered right after she was born, the nurse handed her to me, and Lee kissed my forehead and whispered, "Surprise."

I smiled at the memory and realized that I could remember without the gut-wrenching pain.

That was progress.

Sam had hooked an iPod up to speakers and started a Halloween playlist. The *Ghostbusters* theme. *Time Warp. Thriller.* When *Monster Mash* started to play, he came up behind me. "May I have this dance?"

He took me in his arms and started to slow dance. It wasn't really a dance, more a hold-me-close-and-turn-in-a-circle sort of thing. "I couldn't dance before I messed up my leg," he whispered in my ear.

Then he laughed. And I laughed too as we turned awkward circles together in the center of the bar. "This is tonight's one-thing," I told him. "And it's a very good thing."

"It is," he agreed.

I nodded. I knew that I'd pull this particular memory out in the future, and it would always make me smile.

Chapter Thirteen

The next morning, I took Angus for a long walk up the road.

There was a small church about a half mile up the road at the corner. When the kids were younger, we attended services there when we spent time at camp in the summer.

It was a very small congregation, but they'd been nice people. The minister had been ancient. Gracie always said he looked like Santa and the twins would torment her about still believing in Santa.

Today, as Angus and I walked by, they were singing at the Sunday morning service.

I stood a moment and listened. I recognized the song. *I Love to Tell the Story*.

I remembered going to church when I was nine or ten and singing that song. It was my grandmother's small church in Wesleyville. I spent a lot of weekends with her and we'd go together. She'd hold my hand and sing with gusto, not caring that her voice was off-key. And it was definitely off-key. My father used to joke that she couldn't hit a tune if it were the broadside of a barn.

I hadn't thought of my grandmother in years.

I'd called her Nana and she used to make me tea in a battered yellow teapot and tell me stories.

Part of me wanted to leave Angus tied to a tree and sneak inside and sing along.

I missed church, I realized.

I hadn't known that before, but now, I did. I missed it.

After my grandmother passed away, I didn't go to church regularly. Neither of my parents was active in their church and never pushed the issue. But when I'd had kids, I'd decided to make church a part of our lives. When they were small, we'd all go together. Lee and I would split the kids. One twin, Lee, Gracie, me, the other twin. It saved a lot of fighting.

When the kids got older, I'd leave for church twenty minutes or so before the rest of the family. I'd sit in our pew and just be. I didn't verbalize a prayer, or make requests. I just sat with God. I'd think of everything I was thankful for. I'd count my blessings. And I'd just enjoy those few moments of quiet communion.

Then Lee and the kids would arrive and slide into the pew. We sat between kids. Our strategy didn't always work. Still, I didn't mind. I had those quiet moments before they arrived to sustain me.

And I missed them.

Then I remembered one terrible time as I sat by myself in a pew, not communing, but commanding. Begging. Bartering.

God had ignored me and I hadn't talked to him since.

But maybe it was time to start.

The words of that song played over and over again as I walked Angus back home. "It satisfies my longing, as nothing else can do."

The next day, I knew my one-thing before I left for the bar. I was a bit nervous, wondering if seeing Sam outside the bar, outside of Monday—first on our picnic, then at the party—would change anything, though at this point I was pretty sure it wouldn't. Mondays were magic.

Sam smiled as I walked in and he started drawing my Guinness.

I sat on my barstool and simply enjoyed the moment of quiet.

Drawing a Guinness isn't quite the same as pouring any other brew. It's an art form, and it takes a few minutes.

But I used that time to simply enjoy the quiet murmurs of the bar.

The people talking.

Glasses clinking.

Joanie the waitress, bustling about, delivering food, taking orders.

Jerry at the end of the bar, sipping his Guinness.

Sam came to the end of the bar with a beautiful glass of Guinness and said the words, "One thing."

Picnics and parties hadn't changed anything. It was Monday, this was Sam, and I knew my one-thing.

"Gracie believed in Santa Claus . . ."

"Mom, it's so embarrassing." Connie was not a morning person. Today, she stomped into the kitchen and sat down at her empty cereal bowl. She poured a healthy amount of cereal from the Cheerios box and smothered it in milk.

Gracie followed close on her heels and said, "Morning, Mom."

"What's so embarrassing?" Lexie had found that Connie managed her tribulations better if she had a chance to vent. She'd decided that her job was as Mom the venting precipitator.

"Gracie." Connie's voice was filled with big-sister disgust. She used the same tone when complaining about Conner's room, which frequently was in danger of being condemned by the health department. "Mom, she was talking about Santa yesterday and Julie overheard her. Do you know how embarrassing that was for me?"

As a fourth grader, Connie had reached the upper tier of the elementary school, and Gracie, as a third grader, was embarrassing when she simply breathed.

"Now, Connie—" Lexie started.

Connie interrupted her by leaning across the table and shouting, "There is no such thing as Santa. Mom and Dad buy all the presents."

Gracie didn't look the least bit dismayed as she ate her cereal.

Lee walked into the kitchen, and Connie saw a new place to vent frustration. "Dad, tell Gracie there's no Santa."

"There's no Santa," he echoed.

Lexie kicked him softly. "Lee, we agreed—"

"We agreed that we'd let the kids discover the truth on their own, but it sounds as if Gracie's discovered the truth. She's just ignoring it. She's eight, Lex. That's old enough to accept the way things are. Life's not always the way we want it."

"Gracie, honey, I'm sorry . . ." Lexie said softly.

Rather than look dismayed, Gracie smiled and patted her hand. "It's okay, Mom. I know there's no real Santa. Remember that little girl in the book you read me? That newspaper guy told her that it's okay if moms and dads bought the presents, 'cause they had Santa in their heart. Well, I got him in my heart, too. So, it's okay if Connie don't believe, 'cause I know my heart is big enough for Santa and me."

". . . And that was that. It didn't matter what anyone said; Gracie believed in Santa until the day she died." I tripped over the last word, but managed it. "Every Christmas, she'd leave him cookies. She wrote him annual letters. And when she was twelve, she adopted a family and bought them all gifts with her own money. We all helped, and on Christmas Eve, we packed up everything and put it on their porch. She left a letter with it all—a letter from Santa. We all went back to the car and she was the one who rang the doorbell, then ran."

There was a happy memory that I hadn't pulled out to examine in a long time. Gracie's undisguised glee as she ran to the car.

"She said she was just letting the Santa in her heart out."

"She sounds like she was an amazing girl," Sam said.

"She was. All my kids are."

"Your turn," I said to Sam. "One thing."

"My nickname was Romeo." Sam smiled. "There was this guy in our unit. Tony Mulligan. His dad was Irish, his mom Italian. He was the only swarthy-skinned redhead I ever met . . ."

"Come on, Sam. You're going to be my best man. Consider this part of your duties."

Sam looked at his friend. Tony was one of those guys who never seemed to have it together. He was always late for everything but chow. He was the only guy Sam had ever met who could look rumpled in a newly pressed uniform, and whose hair, no matter how short, looked a mess because of the legion of cowlicks it sported. And the fact that his hair was red only called attention to its disarray. Wherever he went, Tony stood out. And unfortunately, he didn't stand out well.

That is, he didn't stand up well to the scrutiny until he'd met Sheila Yu. Her mother was Irish and her father was Chinese. She was working with an Irish relief agency in Afghanistan. They joked about their future babies, redheaded, tan, blue-eyed babies whose eyes would slant.

"Come with me," Tony pressed.

Going with Tony to ask the CO for permission to marry was about the last thing Sam wanted to do, but Tony looked so desperate, which is why Sam found himself standing before the CO's desk as Tony fumbled his way through his request.

"Listen, Mulligan, you've been in my office weekly, with one infraction or another, since you arrived on this base. What makes you think you're ready to marry?"

"Sir, I . . ."

"Permission to speak freely, sir." Sam heard the words come out of his mouth, but it was as if someone else had said them.

"Permission granted."

"Sir, I know what you're saying. Mulligan is one of the worst soldiers I've ever met. He's the only man I know who can't keep the beat. Not any kind of beat. When he marches, he's always just a bit off. Not enough to get in trouble, but enough that everyone notices."

"You're not helping, Sam," Tony muttered.

Sam ignored him and continued. "Frankly, he sucks as a soldier. But not with Sheila. If you saw them together, sir, you'd know. She . . ." He struggled, looking for the words to explain what he knew—what everyone who'd ever seen Tony and Sheila together knew.

"Sir, there's a line from *Jerry Maguire* that's been so overused that even a guy like me has heard it. She completes him. It's like all those things we've all noticed about Tony are simply signs that he's missing something. It's as if his lack of rhythm when we march and all those other things are just physical manifestations of what's missing. You might think it's a drive to succeed or even caring about his personal appearance, but sir, what's been missing is Sheila. You said Tony's been in here every week, but in the last few months, has he really?"

The CO paused and considered. "No, not recently."

"Not since Sheila."

"So you're saying I should give him permission to marry because it would be good for the unit?"

"In part. But sir, the real reason you should give him permission to marry is that no one should have to go through life missing a part of themselves. I've seen you with your wife, sir, and I know you know what I mean."

❦

"So, what did he say?" Jerry asked from the end of the bar.

"He said, 'Romeo, you have a point.' He gave Tony and Sheila permission and even helped Tony out with the paperwork. Marrying a non-American when you're overseas on assignment means tons of paperwork. And he gave me my nickname. You see, Tony was also lacking an inner sensor. The story of my impassioned speech on his behalf became his favorite bar story. It was less than a week later when the entire base started calling me Romeo."

"You're a romantic." That was something I hadn't known about Sam.

"When I was in a coma, my mother read to me every day. Her favorite books were those Harlequin romances. I blame her."

I couldn't help but ask, "What about the love scenes? That had to be awkward."

He raised his hand. It reminded me of my students. "She read them to me while I was

138

in a coma. Thankfully, I don't remember the stories."

He paused and added, "I'd say I'd ask her if she skipped the love scenes, but I don't think I want to know."

We both laughed. So did Jerry at the end of the bar. And I thought I heard a few other chuckles from nearby tables.

I knew our stories jumped around our personal timelines, but . . . "But this was before you were in the hospital, wasn't it?" I asked. "Your mother's choice of reading material couldn't have influenced your plea on Tony's behalf."

Sam sighed. "I was hoping you wouldn't notice that part."

"Hey, Romeo, I need a refill," Jerry called from the other end of the bar.

Sam groaned. "Mulligan's not even here and he's still torturing me."

He filled Jerry's glass, then came back to me. "So, about a date? How about dinner and a movie on Wednesday? We can go into Erie and . . ."

I nodded, agreeing. I left Sam my number, in case his plans changed for whatever reason, and he gave me his as well. After all these months, we'd never exchanged numbers.

The small scrap of paper felt heavy in my coat's pocket as I walked home.

It was November and chilly. Most of the leaves had fallen and the few diehards that still clung to the trees rustled in the evening breeze, along with the dried cornstalks in a farmer's field. There was the scent of autumn in the breeze as well. The smell of rotting leaves and a potential frost. Of Amish fires, warming their farmhouses. Of animals in pens.

It was cold enough that I'd shoved a knit hat on my head and kept my hands in my coat's pockets. There were gloves rolled up against my hands, but I didn't put them on. Once you started wearing gloves, you might as well admit it was winter. I wasn't ready to admit that yet.

Tonight, I was filled with a warmth that belied the cold. I thought about my date with "Romeo" and smiled. I wasn't sure where this thing with Sam would lead, but I was okay with the uncertainty. He warmed me. After spending so long in the cold, that was enough.

Chapter Fourteen

My first official date with Sam had been uneventful, but nice. He'd remembered that I liked action flicks and taken me to see one with a number of explosions and near misses. As we left the theater, I'd teased him.

"I was afraid you were going to take me to some sappy chick flick, Romeo."

He tried to scowl, but couldn't quite pull it off, and we'd both ended up laughing.

That was the theme of the dinner, too. No talk of painful pasts, just a lot of laughter. I knew that years from now, I'd probably forget what we ate, or even what movie we'd seen. What I'd remember was the laughter and how good it had felt.

I'd carried the feeling with me the rest of the week. I worked on a new square on my tapestry—a Shakespearean mask. It was an obscure reference to Romeo. Probably no one else would understand it but me, but this tapestry was for me. It was a total narcissistic homage to my life. And this square made me smile as I worked on it.

At lunchtime the following Monday, as I reheated a bowl of soup, I realized I hadn't felt the slightest pinch of pain since that date with Sam.

I thought of Lee with nothing but a warm sense of nostalgia.

I was pretty sure I'd reached the tipping point.

I wasn't sure if that's what a psychiatrist would call it, but I knew it existed. Maybe not *it*—not just one point—but *they*, many points. There are moments in the grief process when you make progress. A tipping point. Maybe some grief was so great it took more than one tipping point.

After my father died, my tipping point came that day with my mother at his headstone, then the beach. I still missed him, but the overwhelming grief was gone.

I remembered the moment I'd reached it after Gracie, and I knew I had my one-thing for Sam tonight.

I went to the bar that night, ready to share.

He passed me my Guinness and said, "One thing?"

"One morning, after Gracie died, right before the twins left for college, Connie and Conner were arguing . . ."

"What's going on now?" Lexie stared at her eighteen-year-old twins. They looked so adult, but moments before had sounded very much like they had in grade school when they argued. And whatever was going on now was a kicker of an argument.

Neither answered. "Well, you can tell me, or we can wait and all tell your father about it."

"Dad's been down lately, Mom. We don't want to bother him with this. It was noth—"

"It wasn't nothing. Connie was eavesdropping again." Oceans of frustration flooded Conner's voice.

"Connie?" Lexie asked.

"I wasn't. I just couldn't help overhearing lame-o here with his girlfriend. Oh-Lainy-mm-mm-mm." The *mm* sounds were obviously supposed to represent Conner blowing kisses over the phone.

Lexie tried to look stern, but a smile kept creeping around the edges of her frown. She didn't say anything, sure that if she did, she wouldn't be able to hold back her laughter.

But Connie saw it. "Look, even Mom's laughing."

"I'm not; I'm frowning," Lexie maintained. But in so doing, she'd talked, and her laughter wouldn't be contained. A short, hiccup-length burst broke free.

"Mom." Conner's voice contained volumes of disgust.

"Sorry," Lexie said, and another burst of laughter squeaked out.

This time, Connie didn't comment, she just laughed as well.

And finally Conner joined in. "Man, the only thing that would have made this worse was if Gracie had been here. She'd have started singing that song."

"Oh, yes, she would have. So, in honor of Gracie," Connie said, "Conner and Lainy sitting in a tree. K-I-S-S-I-N-G. First comes love, then comes marriage, then comes Conner with a baby carriage."

All three of them continued laughing as Connie teased Conner and vice versa. The fight had blown over and all that was left was good-natured teasing.

Lexie watched the twins as they ate their breakfast. Soon they'd be gone. Her two Cons, going to different schools and starting independent lives. She wouldn't have to break up any more morning fights. The house would be quiet. Just her and Lee.

Once, they'd talked about those years with anticipation. They'd looked forward to time alone, exploring what it was to be a couple. Now?

"Today is definitely going in my Grace Book," Connie stated more to herself than to Lexie when Conner ran upstairs to get his book bag.

"Grace Book?" she asked.

Connie looked a little embarrassed, but nodded. "Yeah. I started a notebook where I wrote down all kinds of stories about Gracie. I put some pictures in, too. It made me feel better, and I figured someday I might have kids and they won't get to meet Gracie, but I can let them read the book and they'll know something about her. It will make her real to them."

"May I look at the book?"

"Sure, Mom. You can add stories to it, too, if you want."

"That evening, after dinner, Connie brought me down her Grace Book, and I started reading her memories of her sister. I entered a memory of my own that night and as I wrote about Gracie's antics, I laughed. And I realized I'd passed the tipping point. My memories might not beat out the pain, but I could sometimes smile at a thought of Gracie. I don't think a mother can ever totally recover from losing a child, but that night I started to heal. I think I finished my healing process here, with you."

Sam seemed flustered by that and simply asked, "Did you continue to write in Connie's Grace Book?"

"Yes. She left it out after that. Even Conner wrote in it. Connie took it with her when she went to college, but sometimes, I think of a Grace story and email it to her and she adds it."

I hadn't seen the Grace Book in a long time and I suddenly felt an urge to read it again.

I'd call Connie and ask her to bring it next time she came to visit. Maybe for Thanksgiving.

"One thing," I said to Sam.

"The bar in Pittsburgh finished what Grid had started. I finally came back to life. But my life wasn't in Pittsburgh. I told my mother I was leaving Pittsburgh and moving here . . ."

※

"Sam, sweetie, you look great," his mother said in her customary greeting.

Sam figured he could walk in with a full-blown case of the flu and her greeting would be the same, because after seeing him comatose and then in recovery, anything else was gravy.

"So do you, Mom." He kissed her cheek and followed her into the living room. She'd called and asked him to come over, which worked out well for him, because he'd planned on calling her anyway. He'd put off telling her his plans because he knew she wasn't going to be happy, and he figured he'd given his mother enough unhappiness for one lifetime.

"Mom, I wanted to—" he started, but she interrupted.

"Sam, it's been a long time since your father died. Since then it's been just the two of us. But, as you know, I've been dating for a while now and Richard and I are planning to get married." She said the words in a rush, as if afraid of his reaction.

Sam had watched his mother with Richard, and the news wasn't exactly a surprise. " 'Bout time he made an honest woman of you," he teased, then hugged her. "Congratulations, Mom."

She let out a long exhale, as if she'd been holding her breath.

She'd been nervous, Sam realized. "Really, Mom, I'm so happy for you."

This time she sighed, but it didn't sound like nerves. It sounded more like contentment. She smiled then. "He's coming over in a bit. He wants to ask your permission, which I know must seem old-fashioned, but he likes you, Sam."

"And I like him. Seriously, I'm happy for you, Mom. He's a lucky man." He figured there would never be a better time, so he added, "And I hope you'll be happy for me. I bought a bar."

"You bought a bar?"

"Well, I discovered that I'm a pretty good bartender. People seem to like talking to me. But I'm not really satisfied working for someone else forever, so I bought a bar."

"I thought maybe you'd go back—" she started.

He cut her off. "There's no going back for me, Mom. Buying the bar is about moving on to the future."

She didn't react for a minute as she digested

that, then finally she nodded. "Well, moving into the future is great." She was poised to hug him.

He quickly added, "It's not in Pittsburgh, though."

His mother's arms fell back to her side. "Where is it?"

"South of Erie. Less than two hours from your place. Close enough to visit whenever you want. I promise to get a place with a guest room for you and Richard."

At her fiancé's name, her face brightened. "I guess we're both moving on."

"But never moving away from each other. I love you, Mom."

"I love you too, Sam."

❧

"Mom and Richard will be here for Thanksgiving," he said. "I'd like you to meet them."

I nodded. "I'd like to meet them, too. I mean, it's only fair. You've met my mom."

"Speaking of your mom," Jerry said from the far side of the bar. "You ever bringing her back in?"

I nodded. "I'm betting we can talk her into it."

"Why don't you invite her to Thanksgiving?" Sam offered. "Your kids, too, if you think they'd come."

"Thanksgiving?"

Jerry chuckled. "I think the boy is inviting you to Thanksgiving, too. He just neglected to include that part."

Sam rolled his eyes at Jerry. "Of course, you're invited, too. Since Mom and Richard are coming, I thought I'd put together a traditional Thanksgiving dinner here at the bar for anyone who doesn't have somewhere else to go. I could use a hand. That was a hint," he added in case I missed it.

"Lucky for you, I have two hands that don't need much of a hint."

I walked home that night and it felt like it could snow at any moment. There's a certain crispness that hits right before the snow. The ground felt crunchier under my feet and there wasn't a cloud overhead, just a black, black night sky filled with stars and a half-moon.

I could see my breath in the moonlight and I was thankful I'd worn my heavy wool socks. I'd have to pull out my boots soon, not just because of the potential snow, but simply for the warmth.

I watched my breath come out in vivid puffs and felt a sense of anticipation. I'd call Mom and the kids tomorrow. It wouldn't be a traditional Thanksgiving, but somehow I didn't think they'd mind. I knew I didn't.

Chapter Fifteen

That week, I was happy. I added a picture of The Corner Bar to the tapestry. I wasn't sure why I hadn't added it before. It had become a very important part of my life.

No, it was more than the bar. It was the people. Sam. Jerry. Joanie, the waitress and occasional cook. She never really waited on me. To be honest, I'd hardly noticed her until recently. She'd flitted at the edges of the bar, steering clear of Sam and me on Mondays.

I realized that everyone gave us a wide berth and I knew it wasn't because they wanted a barrier between us, but rather it was because they were being considerate of Sam and me.

I hadn't noticed the others until lately. It was as if I was so focused on Sam and our one-things that I hadn't taken in the rest of the bar. But now, working on the picture of its exterior, I was very much aware that there were more people inside than just Sam and me.

That awareness stuck with me on Monday. I waved at Joanie, who was serving a table at the back of the bar, and I gave Jerry a friendly chuck on the shoulder as I walked by. "Mom said she'd come to Thanksgiving. The kids, too."

His eyes lit up. "I'm glad."

I was, too. I was glad that I was here, in this bar, surrounded by friends. I was glad it was Monday. I know most people groan on Mondays because their weekend is over and they have to get back to whatever their work is. When I was teaching, I'd occasionally contract a case of Monday-morning-itis. But when I'd moved to the cottage, there'd been nothing to separate the days. No school days and weekends. No church on Sundays. One day had simply bled into another.

Until I started coming to The Corner Bar.

I'd been in limbo and now . . .

Sam slid a Guinness my way as I took my stool.

"Look, you put a little shamrock in the foam."

"I worked on it all week."

"You've got mad Guinness skills, Sam."

"One thing?" he asked amicably.

I hadn't come with a topic in mind, but looking at the Guinness, I knew what I wanted to say. "Lee and I gave our marriage another chance. We dated and then one day, he said, 'Let's make it official,' and we went down to the courthouse and were married again. Just the two of us, a judge, and some staff who served as witnesses."

"Not the kids?"

I shook my head. "Lee said that our marriage before had been about the kids; now it was time to be selfish, to make it about us. He asked where I'd like to go on a second honeymoon and I answered without hesitation—Ireland. We planned on spending two weeks there.

"It was summer vacation for me, so I could do it, but I worried about Bernie. I wanted to see if Connie or Conner would come home and stay with him, but my mother offered to take the dog. She wasn't happy to see me back with Lee, but she said she wanted to show her support."

"She loves you," Sam said.

I nodded. "So we got married at the court-house; then we went to Ireland."

※

The small white cottage stood nestled on Glenariff Glen. Lexie could see the sea from the house. Lee said things smelled fishy, but Lexie thought the entire area smelled of the sea and of magic—of new beginnings and hope. She reveled in it.

They planned to use the cottage as a home base and branch out from there to explore the Irish countryside. Her family was from the area.

A grandfather, five generations removed, had come from here.

They walked through Glenariff Forest Park every day. There was a long trail, with a wooden bridge walkway. Lexie felt almost content as they stood, looking at the small waterfall.

Only almost content because there was some niggling little worry at the back of her mind. It didn't matter what they were doing; it was there. She couldn't pinpoint exactly what it was. On the surface things were good. But she found herself watching Lee for signs of that changing.

Lexie pushed away her worry and concentrated on the waterfall. It was spectacular. She'd been to Niagara Falls any number of times in her life, since Buffalo was only a few hours away. This was not that kind of waterfall. It was small and surrounded by rocks and foliage.

"It's so green." The words were just a whisper on an exhale.

"Do you want to go somewhere today?" Lee asked. "Giant's Causeway? The cemetery? You know there are Morrows there. You always said you wanted to look for your past here."

She took his hand and realized why she hadn't started looking, hadn't started doing any of the things she'd planned on doing. "I don't want to look at the past today. Not mine. Not ours. Not even distant family members. I want to look to the future, Lee."

"I want . . ." He let the sentence fade away.

"You want?"

"You. I want you."

He took her hand and led her back into the cottage, and for the first time in a long time, they made love. Oh, they'd had sex, but not like this. Not . . .

⟁

I let the sentence trail off. "I'm sorry."

I was embarrassed. I treated my Mondays as if they were private. Just talks between me and Sam. But there was Jerry at the end of the bar and off-and-on others within earshot.

Plus, I was pretty sure that it was bad form to talk to someone you were dating about making love to someone from your past.

"Lexie, we all know you and Lee probably made love."

"You had three kids, after all," Jerry yelled helpfully from the end of the bar.

"You're not helping," Sam barked at Jerry, then smiled at me. "Go on."

"Things were better. Two days later . . ."

⟁

"Come on, lazy bones." Lee smacked her backside for emphasis. "We can't stay in this bed for the entire trip."

"Why not?" Lexie asked.

"We're in Ireland," was his response, as if that, in and of itself, answered her question.

"We're newlyweds," she protested. "People expect us to spend all our time in bed."

Lee laughed and she thought maybe she was imagining that something was off. Those little niggles of nervousness about Lee were nothing. Everything was all right.

"We're the longest-married newlyweds in history. Come on."

They bummed around town, taking in the sights, then ended up at a small cemetery next to the church. They walked, hand in hand, up and down the rows of headstones looking for Morrows. They walked together as if they weren't a couple who'd been married for most of their adult lives. They walked through the past—through rows of old headstones and newer ones. They walked among some headstones that were so old she couldn't make out the names.

There was some commotion at the end of the cemetery, a couple of guys wheeling some machine just beyond the cemetery fence.

"Morning," Lee called. "What's going on?"

"We're looking for the babies," the man nearest to them said.

Lexie must have looked as confused as she felt, because the man clarified. "Unbaptized babies. Years ago, they didn't want them buried in consecrated ground because their souls weren't destined for heaven. There are mass graves out here and the mums are up in arms, so we're extending the boundary of the cemetery to include the wee ones."

"The wee ones," she murmured as she thought about Gracie, about holding her throughout her illness. Gracie had been buried in the cemetery next to Lexie's father, in her mother's very practical extra plot. But she didn't think of Gracie and that small stone that marked her resting place.

No, when she thought of Gracie, she thought about her alive and laughing. Reading books together. Like snapshots in an album, Lexie saw her. On the garage roof with her siblings. Sneaking halfway down the stairs after bedtime and stealing a few extra minutes of television.

She saw snapshots of Gracie with ease in her mind. She'd had that time with her daughter.

"I got to hold Grace," she said. "I got to hold her, and I have memories. I know where she's buried and can visit. But these moms . . ." Lexie started to cry for the babies whose souls weren't destined for heaven. For the babies who hadn't been allowed to rest in consecrated ground. "These moms don't even have a headstone to visit. Nothing. No memories. No burial site. Nothing but a hole in their heart that never truly heals."

❧

"I'm not sure why it bothered me so much, but it did. We finally got up and walked back into town. We stopped at the pub and I had a Guinness. We talked about Gracie as we drank. Listening to the men talk about babies being buried in unconsecrated soil seemed horrible to me. But there, in the pub afterward, we talked about our past, about what we hoped to find in our future.

"Lee and I talked as I drank Guinness. For the first time, we talked with ease about the daughter we lost. We talked about our life together, even our divorce. We cleared the air and said so many things that needed to be said out loud. When I first came here and asked for it, it was because Guinness reminds me of comfort."

"Then I'm doubly glad I ordered it in. If I'd known, I'd have ordered it sooner."

"Now, when I drink it, it's not just comfort; it's a gift. Every time you bring me a pint of Guinness, that feeling of comfort is augmented by a feeling of . . ." I shrugged. I didn't know how to put it into words. But it was there. Every time Sam brought me a pint, I felt a warmth. His gift of Guinness reminded me that despite the dark days, I'd found Sam. A friend. A place to belong.

"I don't know how to explain," I finally said. "But you're there, too. Mixed into that feeling. Thank you for that."

"I do know what you mean about a certain thing having a feeling associated with it. For me it's birdseed."

"Birdseed?" I wanted to laugh and one look at Sam's grin, I knew it was okay. "All right, I think we're all waiting to see what sort of feeling birdseed evokes for you."

"When Mom and Richard got married, I was the . . ."

◎◎

Sam walked his mother to the front of the church. She was wearing an ivory skirt and jacket. He'd have said white, but his mother had assured him it was ivory. Since her son was going to be there, everyone would know she shouldn't be wearing white.

Sam had pointed out she should wear whatever she wanted, and she'd assured him she was. She was wearing ivory.

They reached the front of the church and Richard was there waiting for his mom. Sam put his mother's hand in Richard's, then, rather than sitting down, he'd simply moved to one side.

He'd tried to talk his mother out of making him her maid of honor, but she wouldn't hear of anyone else doing it. He'd begged her to call him her man of honor and she'd obliged, but every time she'd said the words, he'd known she was thinking maid of honor.

158

"Wait, wait," Jerry called from the end of the bar, pulling Sam from his one-thing. "You mean, you were your mother's maid of honor?"

"Man of honor," Sam repeated.

"Oh, Romeo," Jerry teased.

It wasn't only Jerry and me laughing. A number of the patrons were obviously listening because there was a distinct laughter coming from the nearby tables. And Joanie, the waitress and sometimes cook, didn't even attempt to disguise the fact she was listening. She sat down on the stool next to me.

Sam gave her a significant look, one I might have used on the kids when they were young, but Joanie just grinned and stayed put.

"Don't listen to them, Sam," I said. "I think it's lovely your mom asked you to be her ma—" That *A* had started out with a long sound, but I quickly changed it to a short *A* and finished, "man of honor. Tell me about the birdseed."

"The ceremony was short and to the point; then my mom and Richard walked down the aisle and I followed with his brother, who was his best man . . ."

Sam walked through the receiving line and hugged his mother. "Just be happy, Mom," he whispered in her ear.

"How could I not be happy? I'm married to Richard and you're home, safe and healthy. Now, if we could just work on the happy for you."

"Well, I have enough happiness today to share some with you, Sam," Richard said, taking his hand and shaking it, then pulling him into a hug. "I thought I'd grow old a well-established bachelor, but now, I'm not only married, but I've gained a son—that is if you don't mind?"

Sam didn't remember his father, but he remembered dreaming of one when he was young. Someone who cared about him, who'd show up at his games and graduations. Someone who'd maybe teach him to fish, or drive. Just a regular dad, like so many of his friends had.

Richard definitely wasn't the fishing sort, and Sam had long since learned to drive, but he had a feeling he'd be the kind of man to show up at events, or to show up just because Sam asked him to. "I'd be honored, sir . . . Dad."

The rest of the small assembly of friends and family filed through the line and shook hands with the happy couple and with Sam and Richard's brother.

Then his mom and Richard ran out the door of the chapel into a barrage of birdseed that flew from the guests' hands. His mom's ivory suit was covered. Bits of it clung to her hair. But his normally impeccable mother didn't mind at all. She took Richard's hand and got in the limo. Before it pulled away, she looked at Sam and mouthed the words, *I love you.*

◯◯

"My mom gained a husband that day, the kind of husband she'd always deserved, and I got a father. Wait until you meet him. I think you'll agree that Richard was worth the wait."

"Did he ever take you fishing?"

Sam laughed. "He's not the fishing kind of guy. Richard's about six inches shorter than my mom and . . . I guess I'd describe him as tweedy. When you read a book and there's a character who's an English professor, Richard is the guy you picture."

"Is he an English professor?"

"History, actually."

"I'd better check my tables." Joanie got up from her stool and started the rounds in the quiet tables.

"He sounds wonderful, Sam."

"You'll see for yourself on Thanksgiving."

I thought about tonight's one-things as I walked home in the cold. For me, Guinness meant a quiet comfort after an upset. It meant companionship. Birdseed meant love to Sam.

Maybe family. Oh, he hadn't said either thing, but he didn't need to.

I realized that each picture on my tapestry was like tonight's one-things. Symbols that carried some memory or feeling. A doe and three fawns. A graduation cap. A woman being licked by a giant dog. The Corner Bar. Each was just a symbol. Each represented something in my life.

The tapestry as a whole represented my healing.

After my time alone in the cottage, I was ready to start living life again.

There were a few more things to share and then maybe I'd be ready to move on. No, not ready. I knew I was ready. Able. I needed to tell the last pieces of the story, in order to be able to truly move forward.

If you'd asked me even a few months ago, I'd have said no . . . I couldn't recover this time. I'd found a way beyond my father's death and Gracie's, but this time I hadn't been sure I had it in me.

I still wasn't sure, but I felt hopeful.

It had been a long time since I'd felt hope.

It was like an old friend whom I'd missed.

And that was something.

Chapter Sixteen

I'd spent Tuesday and Wednesday working on a new tapestry block. A glass of Guinness surrounded by birdseed.

I wasn't exactly sure anyone else would know it was birdseed. I'll confess, it looked more like polka dots on a tablecloth under the beer. But I knew. And since this piece was all about me and for me, that's what mattered.

For years, I'd worked to perfect my crafts. I could weave a basket. I could crochet an afghan. I could make a quilt. I could paint a decent picture. I could teach any and all, though none were my medium of choice. Pottery was. I hadn't made anything in a very long time. After losing Gracie, I'd lost the urge to create.

When I was in the classroom I'd graded more about the passion a student had for a project than for his or her execution. The passion was the most important part of creating for me. I thought my passion for my craft was gone forever, but I felt that old familiar drive about my tapestry. When it was done, I thought I might rediscover my drive for my pottery.

Connie came in Wednesday night for Thanksgiving and slept at the cottage. I'd asked, so she brought the Grace Book with her. I thumbed through the pages, reliving the memories with Connie. We laughed at a few and cried at others.

Conner and Mom drove in together from Erie on Thursday and we all met at Sam's.

The bar was bustling with people, many of whom I recognized. Joanie and Jerry, of course, but also the couple who frequently came in on Mondays and sat at one of the back tables. A few other guys who met at the bar before bowling.

I introduced Connie, Conner, and my mom around. Mom and Jerry went to work back in the kitchen. They were making pumpkin pies, each boasting that their pie recipe was the best. The kids started to set up tables. A little girl sat at one of the tables. "Hi, honey. Who are you?"

"Molly. My mom's . . ." She pointed at Joanie, the waitress. "We're gonna eat here today. Mr. Sam said I can have the drumstick."

"Molly, you remind me of my girls when they were little."

"I'm not little," she insisted with all her five- or six-year-old might.

I nodded seriously. "Sorry. You're right; you're not little at all."

I pitched in, setting up the tables so they lined up to form one long table. I covered each with mismatched tablecloths. Sam had a box filled with gourds and ornamental corn and I arranged some as a centerpiece.

Connie came up behind me and put an arm over my shoulder. "Lookin' good, Mom."

"You worked at it, too."

"I'm not talking about the table. I'm talking about you. You look good. Better than you have in a long time. What's changed?"

I knew she was asking a serious question, but today wasn't about serious, it was about family—about giving thanks. So rather than answer, I hugged her. "A new haircut. You know what they say, a good one can make all the difference."

She didn't try to get more out of me; she just grinned and said, "Then next time I'm in town, make me an appointment at your salon."

A while later, the door opened and a stranger walked into the room. Sam was still in the back cooking, so I went over to greet him. "Welcome."

"Is Sam around?"

"He's in the back. Let me go back and get him for you."

I didn't need to go back. Sam came out of the kitchen and the stranger hollered, "Romeo!"

"Grid?" I said, more to myself than to him.

But he heard me. "Do I know you?"

When Sam had talked about Grid, I'd pictured a huge man, someone straight from some military movie. Tall, buff, hard looking. Instead, Grid wasn't much taller than my five feet, five inches. And he looked like a man who was quick to smile.

"No, but I know you. Thanks for everything you did for Sam." I didn't say anything more because the two men were hugging each other, in that guy way that involved a lot of backslapping, as if to prove they were manly, despite the display of affection.

"I brought someone along with me." The door opened again and a stunning woman came in, followed by a short, squattish, very bald man.

"Mom, Richard," Sam said. This time the hugging didn't involve backslapping. "I want you all to meet everyone. Starting with Lexie. A good friend."

Three sets of eyes studied me, as if weighing what precisely Sam meant by "good friend." I didn't know that I could have come up with a better definition myself.

People mixed and visited. My mother sat at a booth talking to Sam's mom, while Richard and Jerry sat at the bar watching some football pregame on the television.

My kids were chatting with Joanie—Connie had Molly on her lap.

I stood in the corner, just watching everyone and feeling this warmth practically spill over me. Then Sam was standing next to me. "I'd say it was a pretty good party," he said.

I looked up at him, my 'good friend,' and took his hand in mine. "The best."

An hour and a half later, the long table was filled with friends, family, and Sam. I wasn't sure exactly where he fit. He was more than a friend, but not quite family. He was . . . Sam. I decided that was enough of a definition.

"Before we start eating, I thought we'd all go around the table and name what we're thankful for," Sam said. "I'll start. New friends. Old friends. Family."

Friends and family was the theme as everyone went around. Molly switched things up a bit because she was thankful for pumpkin pie and drumsticks—in that order.

I was sitting next to Sam, who'd started at the opposite side, so I was last. "Like everyone else, I'm thankful for friends and family—those who are here with us and those who aren't. And I'm thankful for onething."

Sam turned and smiled at me. Jerry, across the way, smiled as well. Some of the regulars understood. Joanie did. But my family and

Sam's looked confused. None of us enlightened them. It was a private thing.

A bar thing.

A Monday thing.

When I looked around me, I realized just how much I had in my life, and I was very thankful for that.

It had been a long time—too long—since I'd considered that.

Chapter Seventeen

I stood on the back porch, a steaming cup of coffee in my hand. It was too early for Angus, who hadn't budged when I got up.

It was so cold that it was like breathing in . . . Well, ice cubes sounded like the logical analogy, but ice melts and its ragged edges smooth over as it warms. There was no smoothing of the freezing air I inhaled. It scratched at my nose and lungs as I breathed. So, sand. It was so cold it was like breathing in grains of sand.

I stood there in the dark, cold morning and I was very aware of the fact that I was alone out here. Normally Angus was at my side, a bit of life to remind me there was something else out there, but now, it was just me. The nighttime animals had gone to bed, and the daytime ones hadn't begun to really stir yet.

I hugged my sweater to me with my one free hand, and as I did so I realized I was wearing my wool Irish, cable-knit sweater.

I'd bought it at a small corner shop in Dublin. Memories of that trip flooded through me, like a slide show.

I remembered.

I realized I was crying. My tears felt frozen on my cheek. They bit and scratched more than the cold that rattled like so much sand in my lungs.

I remembered and I cried.

When I was too numb to do more of either, I went in with my cup of now-cold coffee, woke Angus, and headed to the workshop. I studied the tapestry on the loom, with its half-finished picture of Guinness on its dots. Normally, I felt driven to finish, but I couldn't bring myself to work on it today. I couldn't think of Ireland and everything that happened after. Not now. Not yet.

Today I needed something fresh. Something that wasn't about the past. I'd spent the last year wallowing in it. I needed something that was about the here and now.

I braved the weekend after Thanksgiving shopping frenzy and went into town to buy some fresh clay.

It felt good to be back at the wheel. This was my true talent—my true art. I learned about and dabbled with other mediums, but pottery . . . I don't know that I can describe it, but it's home. There's something so primal, so tactile about wedging the clay, a sort of kneading motion. Then shaping it into a ball and placing it in the center of the batt.

But what I really love is the forming of

the object. What was once a lump of clay, through the power of my hands and inner vision, becomes something else entirely. A bowl. A plate. A vase. Some might say there's more artistry in the glazing, but to my mind that's just the frosting. It's the pottery itself that's the heart of the creation.

I worked on a bowl. Something small, but substantial. Maybe Sam would like it for peanuts on the bar.

The thought made me smile and I started to sing *Saucy Sailor*. It was an old tune. I wasn't even sure where I'd learned it, but it had a nice beat. They used to tease me in school because I frequently sang as I worked. The rhythm of a song melded with the rhythm of the wheel and my hands.

I'm not sure how long I worked, but Angus barked and pulled me from the song and the bowl.

The door opened and Sam was there. "You were singing."

"I was. It's been a long time since I sang."

"You have a nice voice." He chuckled. "That sounded inane."

"It was a compliment; thanks. What's up?" Talk about inane. What's up?

"I was out running errands and found myself here. I hope you don't mind."

"I don't."

I stood there in my apron, my hands covered with clay, staring at Sam bundled in a winter coat, in boots. "It's snowing?"

"Started early. How long have you been in here?"

"Long enough. Would you like to come up to the cottage?"

"I'd like . . ."

His sentence trailed off as in large, quick strides he covered the space that separated us. I knew what he had in mind and I welcomed it. I met him and his kiss. There, covered in clay, a storm brewing outside, I kissed Sam Corner and something that I'd thought was gone forever was back.

Maybe some things.

There was happiness.

Yearning.

But there was something more than that. I wasn't sure I was ready for it, so I just let that feeling hunker down in a corner and wait.

I was ready, however, to take Sam into my house and into my room.

And there was happiness.

Later that day, I was wearing my favorite Woolrich slippers, a pair of panties, and a soft, button-down denim shirt that was probably another rescued Conner-castoff as I pulled some chicken soup out of the freezer and popped it, frozen, into a pan.

"You're still singing," Sam said as he came up behind me and wrapped his arms around my waist.

"I'm still happy."

"What's the song?"

I had to think a moment about what I'd been mindlessly singing this time. It was the same song. The family used to call that a skip. I'd get a song stuck in my head and like an old vinyl record, keep skipping on it. "It's an old, traditional one. *Saucy Sailor*. It's about a man who's come back from sea and asks his girl to marry him. She turns him down, telling him he's ragged and smelly. When he tells her he has silver in his pocket, she changes her mind, but it's too late. He's going to find another girl to marry." I hummed a few more bars.

"I like it on you."

"The song or the slippers?" I held up my right, red-and-black checked slipper for emphasis.

"The happiness."

It shouldn't surprise me that Sam recognized my current mood. "You helped put it there." He didn't respond to that. "Can I tell you one thing, Sam?"

"Here?"

"It's not really a one-thing. It's just a friend sharing a memory with a friend."

He nodded and just waited in that particularly Sam way of waiting. He waited as if whatever I was about to say was the most important thing in the world to him. As if there was nothing but him and me.

"The last time I remember feeling like this, truly happy . . ."

Lexie laughed as the kids stood at the edge of the water. May on Lake Erie wasn't for the faint of heart. The lake's temperature hovered somewhere in the fifties. When she was young and foolish, she'd skipped school with friends and come here. She could still remember how the water had bitten sharp, stinging nips at her skin as she jumped in with them.

"Come on, Mom," Conner called.

"I'm too old to be that foolish. You all go ahead." But instead of jumping in the water, the three of them came and grabbed her hands, pulling her from the blanket. "No, seriously. I'm not getting in that water. It's too cold. I'm too old . . ."

The kids paid no attention to her protests. Conner was almost as tall as his father now, and he pulled on one hand while the two girls teamed up on the other. Dragging her closer and closer to the water's edge.

"I am your mother; you wouldn't." Lexie tried to sound stern, but the kids only laughed harder as they continued to pull. "Kids . . ."

And with that, all four of them were in the water.

The water was sharp and stung at her skin. Lexie cried out, but she wasn't alone. The kids all screamed as well, and all four of them bolted from the water, laughing. Happy, despite the chill.

⚬

"It was so cold that we gathered up our things, got in the car, and turned the heat on, full blast. We rode home and made hot chocolate. Lee came in and found the four of us, huddled under blankets, sipping the cocoa from our mugs and said, 'It's almost seventy degrees outside.'

"The kids and I smiled at each other, sharing the newly formed memory. And I was happy. Bone deep. Complete. I don't think I've been that utterly, contentedly happy since." I paused and embraced him. "Until now."

Sam spent Saturday with me. He said he'd hired a new part-time bartender and he called him in to take care of the crowd. I slept in Sam's arms.

That sounds like a small thing. I went to sleep with someone and slept in his arms. But in a way, sleeping next to Sam was more intimate than making love to him. There's a vulnerability when we sleep. And I'd never slept in any man's arms except Lee's. Even Jensen, who I'd dated so briefly, had never spent a night with me.

I woke up before Sam and watched him sleeping. He needed a shave, but he'd have to wait for that until he went home, unless he could make do with a pink disposable razor and some women's baby oil–scented shaving cream.

On that thought, he woke up. "What's that smile about?"

"I was wondering if you were confident enough in your manhood to shave with a pink razor."

Turns out, he was.

Clean-shaven and bundled up, we took Angus for a long Sunday morning walk.

There were a few inches of snow, and Angus acted as if he'd never seen the stuff before. He galloped through it, he ate it, and finally rolled in it.

There was something so easy about being with Sam like this. We didn't talk, but simply enjoyed the morning in each other's company.

We walked past the church up the road and they were singing. If it had been just Angus and me, I might have stopped to listen, but I didn't. I kept walking and listened to the music slowly fade away as we got farther away, and I tried to ignore the realization that I missed going to services. Maybe soon I'd be ready.

By the time lunch rolled around I felt a headache start to build just behind my eyes. By supper, the headache had exploded and I ached from head to toe and my nose was so congested I could hardly breathe.

Sam tucked me in and spent that night too, but spent it on the couch. He got up periodically to check on me. It had been a long time since someone worried when I had a cold.

"No bar tonight," he proclaimed Monday morning.

"For you or for me?"

"Both of us."

"It's sweet you want to stay with me, but it's just a cold. How about we compromise? I'll give up this one Monday, but you should go to work."

"I could call Chris, the new bartender."

"Or you could go."

"Will you call me if you need anything?"

"It's just a cold, Sam, but I promise I'll call."

He left, still looking concerned. I laid back knowing that if I called, he would rush back to my side.

That was a powerful gift he'd given me.

Chapter Eighteen

As I dozed in my germ-infested isolation on Monday and Tuesday, I dreamed about the Erie house.

Conner's room had a closet that sat right above the stairway, so it was really only half a closet. The floor of it was about two feet off the ground. Since Conner had an aversion to hanging up his clothes, the kids had used it as a play area. That play occasionally included locking one or the other of them up in it.

I dreamed I was locked in the closet and I could hear the family outside the door. I didn't try to get out, but simply leaned back against the slanted back wall and listened. I could hear Gracie out there, laughing with the twins. I could hear Lee.

I dreamed about the claw-footed bathtub. On particularly hard days, the thought of escaping for an hour into a bubble bath was all that kept me going. I dreamed of bubble baths and scented candles. I woke up and could smell the honeysuckle candle I'd used.

On Wednesday I felt almost human, and I knew it was time to clear out the old house. I felt like I was—if not making a new beginning—getting close to making a new beginning. I knew that there were still hurdles to overcome before I could close the door on the past. The house in Erie was one of them.

It had been over a year since I'd been back. I kept it warm enough that the pipes didn't freeze and I paid the bills, but otherwise, I ignored its existence, as if by ignoring it, I could ignore the painful experiences that happened there. But I couldn't outrun those memories by running away from home to the cottage. I was still caught in them. I needed to face them in order to truly be free of them. If I'd learned anything from my Mondays with Sam, it was that ignoring things didn't work.

I called Conner and Connie and asked if they could meet me at the house in Erie that Friday night. They both still had things there that they might want to claim. Plus, I thought this should be a family affair. We'd experienced so much between those walls. We should say good-bye together as well.

I got there early. Although we needed to do this as a family, I needed some time on my own there first.

Glenwood Hills was a lovely section of Erie, just south of Thirty-Eighth Street, one of the main roads through town. The houses were old and predominately brick. The streets were tree-lined. One of the neighbors had shoveled the sidewalk in front of the house and I stomped my way up the still snow-filled stairs.

I pulled the key from my purse and I realized that the keychain felt foreign. Once I'd used it daily, but it had languished in a drawer for so long it had lost that sense of familiar, much like this house itself. I remembered moments in it, but it had ceased feeling like home. The cottage was my home now.

I stood on the stoop, holding the key in my hand.

I'd unlocked this door thousands of times. I'd unlocked it while juggling anything from groceries to babies. I'd unlocked it in every type of weather, thankful for the overhang that sheltered the three steps up and the small stoop.

I slipped the key into the keyhole and turned it. It was a bit sticky, which made sense because it had sat unused for so long.

I put my coat and my boots on the same hook and same spot on the mat that I'd used for years.

I opened the door to the kitchen.

It looked like it always had except the refrigerator was unplugged and the door was propped open. I was surprised that the house wasn't as dusty as I thought it would be. But there was an unfamiliar smell that spoke of disuse, whereas once the house had smelled of countless family meals, pans of brownies, and an occasional wet dog.

The house was silent, where once it had been filled with children's noises. Screams, laughter, loud music.

For a house to be truly a home, there had to be people, smells, and sounds. This was just a house—an empty shell where once there'd been a home.

I stopped at the thermostat and turned up the heat when I went into the dining room; then I continued into the living room. Both looked the same. As if just yesterday the family had eaten dinner around that table, or I'd sat on one side of the couch with Lee on the other as we read or watched something on television.

I was just about to start up stairs, when I heard someone come in the side door. "Mom?" Conner yelled.

I went back into the kitchen as he came in. "You're early."

He grinned. "So are you." Then my son, my joker, grew more serious. "We both figured you'd come early and didn't want you to face this by yourself. Connie'll be here soon. We didn't want you to have to go through things alone."

He took my hand in his and I looked at my son. In my mind's eye, he's still the little boy battling two sisters. Raging because they spied on him. Playing jokes that made them crazy.

That boy was gone. Now a man stood in his place. There was a lot of Lee in his son. The same blue eyes, but my dark hair. It had been lighter when he was young, but now, it was almost the same shade as mine and cut so short it was almost a crew cut.

"Well, since you're here first, you can start."

"What are we doing here tonight, Mom?"

"I want you both—"

The door opened again. Moments later Connie joined us. "It's snowing. Good thing I'm crashing with you tonight, Mom. I wouldn't want to drive back in that."

"You do remember that heading south of Erie means more snow than here by the lake?" I teased.

"Yeah, but a half hour is a lot easier to face than two-and-a-half hours."

"Mom was just telling me what she wants us to do here tonight."

"I want you both to go through everything and anything. Take what you want. If you want furniture, we'll make arrangements for that. I'm taking my personal items and my grandmother's chair, but basically selling whatever else you two don't take."

"Mom . . ." they both said as one.

Before I had the kids, I'd have said that myth about twins completing each other's sentences was just that—a myth. But my two Cons had taught me otherwise. Even though they were adults now and lived in different cities, they still managed to twin-speak on occasion.

"It's time, kids. The house has been vacant for more than a year. I just realized recently that I don't live here anymore. My home is the cottage. This is simply the house I used to live in. It's filled with memories—both happy and sad. But it's not mine anymore. It's just a repository for those memories. And I don't need something physical to hold on to those."

They both looked concerned.

"This isn't something sad. It's me moving on. And I think you'd both agree, it's about time."

They looked at each other, and did their psychic-twin voodoo thing, then nodded.

"So where do we start?" Conner asked for them both.

"Let's start down here."

What might have been a sad thing turned out to be filled with happy nostalgia.

We went through the downstairs. There wasn't much I took. Photos, mainly. My grandmother's rocking chair. I loaded them all into the truck, thankful for the cap on the back.

Then we went upstairs. The kids each went

to their rooms and I went into the room I'd shared for so many years with Lee. The room I'd used on my own while we were separated. The room he'd come back to.

I'd taken most of my clothes with me when I'd started staying at camp. There wasn't much in the room I needed or wanted. My jewelry box. More pictures.

Then I spotted Lee's ugly red sweater on the back of the chair. I'd hated that thing. It was baggy and tattered. I'd threatened to toss it out, but never had the nerve. He'd loved it and never saw a problem with wearing it out in public, but finally the kids ganged up on him with me and he agreed to just wear it around the house.

I put it on my small pile of keepsakes. Then left the room to find the kids. They were standing outside Gracie's closed bedroom door.

"You can go in," I told them.

Connie splayed her fingers against the door, below the small ceramic plaque that proclaimed, GRACIE'S ROOM. "It seems wrong, picking through her things."

"She'd want you both to have something of hers."

They still stood, frozen, so I opened the door and went in. The kids followed behind me.

Conner's arms draped over both my

shoulders and Connie's. "I still miss her," he said.

Connie walked over to Gracie's bed and picked up a Cabbage Patch doll. "Britta Patty. She was my doll for all of two minutes; then Gracie stole her. She loved her more than I ever could."

"Maybe you should take it. Someday you can give it to your daughter."

Connie lifted up the corner of the mattress and pulled out a battered orange blanket. "Only if Conner takes her blankie. Do you remember when we went to Greenfield Village and spent the night at that hotel in Detroit? We got almost an hour toward home before Gracie remembered that she forgot Blankie."

"Remembered she forgot?" Conner teased. Then he joined in the remembrance. "Dad was not pleased about having to drive back."

That was an understatement and we all recognized that. Lee hadn't wanted to drive back, but Gracie's mounting hysteria finally convinced him. The ride had been a white-knuckle one for me, as he drove wildly back to Detroit.

"Take Blankie, Con. Someday you might get some woman drunk enough to agree to procreate with you—that's the only way you'll reproduce. But those kids should know about Gracie."

They were sniping, as always, but I could tell that being in here, in Gracie's room, moved them as much as it moved me. I fingered her bookshelf. "She was my biggest reader."

I pulled out a book. "You two should take some of these." The set of Chincoteague books was on the top shelf. I took them out and put them on the floor; then I pulled out another small stack. "*Belinda*," I said, recognizing Gracie's favorite book.

"*Belinda Mae*," Connie corrected me with a small laugh. "Gracie sang that song for weeks," Connie said. "B-E-L I-N-D A-M-A-E that is me. With Belinda Mae, then Sophia cannot win, Belinda Mae begin again."

I opened the book and a piece of paper fell out.

I picked it up and my hand started to shake as I recognized the handwriting on the envelope: *Mom, Dad, Connie, and Conner.* "It's from Gracie."

The envelope was sealed, so I gently slid my finger underneath it to break the seal, pulled out a piece of notebook paper, and read aloud.

I'm not sure who found this, or how long it took you to find it, but I'm sure someday you will find it. And I am sure that you all will share it, so hello Mom, Dad, Connie, and Con.

I know you were sad when I died.

Yes, despite Mom's attempt to remain upbeat, I know I'm going to die. Dad, when you took us to church a few weeks ago, the minister said something about how he tries to be happy about what he has, rather than sad about what he doesn't. That stuck with me because I've had a wonderful life. I never doubted, not even for a minute, that you all loved me. And I have so many really great memories. Mom yelling at the three of us when she caught us on the garage roof. That time Mom got all sad 'cause we were growing up and so we took her to the zoo in order to make her think we weren't really that old. Remember? The camels were having sex and Mom about had a heart attack, then quick as a minute, she told us that they were just trying to give each other piggyback rides. Mom, it was just last year. We were in our teens, and we all knew what sex was.

Mom, I put the letter in the book because I remember you reading it. I loved that song she used to spell her name, B-E-L I-N-D A-M-A-E that is me. And that time I had chicken pox, you read it to me over and over. And you made me my own song.

Amazing Gracie, has chicken pox, her face is itchy and red, but Mommy is here, and you are dear, so keep your butt in bed.

I didn't realize you'd ripped off Amazing Grace until we were at church at camp and they sang it. I looked at you and we both burst out laughing.

And Dad,

I read the words, and choked up, realizing Lee wasn't here to hear Gracie's letter.

"Mom, they're together now. He knows," Conner said.

I nodded and went back to reading.

And Dad, how about the time you took us all fishing and the crickets got out in the car? Conner had fallen asleep and didn't wake up when we all bolted outside. Mom told you to go rescue him, but there was a huge cricket on his head and you were laughing so hard, you couldn't.

Those are my memories. My whole life has been filled with those kinds of things. I guess they are sort of small things, but they mean everything to me.

And while I'm sad to leave you all, if I could pick living to eighty years with some other family, or spending sixteen years, or maybe I'll make it to seventeen. But however long I make it, if I could pick eighty years with another family or my few years with you all, I'd pick less years with you all every time.

Remember me.

I love you all.

Remember to love each other.

Gracie. God, how I missed her. I tried to imagine what my youngest would look like now as an adult, but I couldn't. In my mind, she would always be a teen. My little Gracie.

"Mom," the twins said in unison.

"I'm fine." I brushed at my face and realized I'd been crying. "I miss her, that's all. I'll always miss her. But I've finally recovered as much as any mother can."

I might figure out how to put my past behind me and recover from the pain, but I realized that I'd never stop missing the people

I loved who'd gone on without me. My father, Gracie, Lee.

We finished going through the house. Connie and Conner both decided to rent a U-Haul and take some furniture. They still had keys and wouldn't need me for that. I'd taken everything I wanted. Whatever was left when they were done, I'd sell; then I'd put the house on the market. I didn't need to come back to it again. My memories were with me and didn't rely on the house.

I took the book and the letter, packed up the car, and told Connie that I'd meet her at the cottage, but I had a quick stop to make first.

Though it wasn't Monday, I stopped at Sam's bar. It was bustling with people.

"Lex?" Sam said by way of greeting as I came in, covered in snow.

My stool was occupied. I mean, I knew other people used it when I wasn't here, but it was still odd to see someone else sitting on it. "One thing," I said. "I know it's busy and this won't take long, but I need to tell you one thing."

He waved at the new bartender, Chris, and he took me into the kitchen. There was a cook there I'd never met. I waved as we continued through it into Sam's office.

I'd never been in here, I realized. I'd never been to Sam's apartment, either. There were still parts of his life I hadn't been introduced to. We sat down on a rather battered plaid couch. The office was just a little worn at the edges, but very neat. A pressboard bookcase had notebooks and some other big, official-looking books and binders on it. His desk was one of those metal ones that you might find in any office. Everything on it was neat and precise.

"One thing," he said, pulling me from my inspection.

I took the letter out of the book and handed it to him. I waited while he read it. "I can recite most of the book by heart. Gracie mentions me reading it to her when she had chicken pox, but that's not the time that stands out in my mind. It was toward the end . . .

"One thing," Sam said again.

⸙

"Mom." Gracie's voice was so low that it was hard to be sure she'd said anything.

"Hey, sleepy head."

"I was just thinking about Belinda Mae. Would you read it to me?"

How Belinda Mae Got Her Name was a children's book and not the kind of book Lexie read to teenaged Gracie most afternoons. But she got it off Gracie's shelf. The floor-to-ceiling built-in was crammed with books. A few years ago, she'd offered to store the children's books, but Gracie had protested, claiming it would be like putting a friend in the attic.

Lexie read the book about Belinda Mae's battle with Sophia, a bossy classmate. In the end, Belinda won the right to be called her whole, very long, name, but in a gesture of generosity, she shared the prize with her classmate. Rather than Belinda Mae Abernathy, she'd simply be Belinda Mae and Sophia could be Sophia Tonya.

Gracie sighed as Lexie finished the story. "When I was little, I thought I wanted to grow up and be like Belinda Mae. She was brave, but she was also kind. I liked that. But a few years ago, I took the book babysitting, and as I read it, I realized that I only wanted to be like Belinda Mae because she reminded me of you. You're so strong, Mom. Brave and kind, like her. If I were going to grow up, I'd have wanted to grow up and be just like you."

Hearing her talk so casually about the idea of not growing up broke Lexie's heart into a thousand pieces. Her voice cracked as she managed, "Gracie, I'm not brave, or strong."

"You're wrong, Mom. You are. But more than that, you love with your whole heart. I know that if you could love me well, I wouldn't be sick now . . ."

i'd choked back the tears as I read the letter with the kids, but I was crying now as I told this one-thing—this one big thing—to Sam. "I couldn't love her well, though. And I realized Gracie was wrong. I'm not any of those things. I'm not brave or strong. Look at how I've fallen apart."

"Lex—"

I interrupted him. I didn't want him to argue, or to tell me I was wrong. "I feel like I let her down. I know it's stupid, that Gracie's been gone a long time, but still, I feel as if I've somehow failed her because I'm not the things she thought I was."

"You didn't ask me my one-thing." There was censure in his voice, not pity.

"Do you have one?"

"After I bought the bar, Grid came to visit for a couple weeks to help get things set up."

❧

"It's going to be a nice place, once you get it cleaned up," Grid said.

Sam looked around the bar, which probably hadn't seen the bristle side of a scrub brush in a couple decades. "Cleaning's about all I can afford. After I got done putting down the money on this, plus the liquor license and the rest of the start-up costs, there's not a lot left for renovations."

"You wouldn't want to do that anyway," Grid assured him. "The decor is part of the charm. Let's just call it historic decor."

"Well, let's hope that the customers think that, because I've got everything tied up in it."

"My thoughts have always been, go big or go home."

Sam knew Grid meant it as a joke, but he didn't laugh. "This could be the dumbest move I've ever made."

"Well, dumb or not, it was brave. That's something to hang your hat on."

"I'm not brave. I think we both know that."

"We do?"

"Look at how you had to come rescue me in the hospital."

"Listen, being brave doesn't mean doing things on your own; it means being smart enough to ask for help when you need it."

"I didn't ask," Sam reminded him.

"Well, sometimes being brave means picking friends who are so smart that they don't need to wait for you to ask."

☙

"I think Gracie would be proud of you. You're here. You came to me tonight and let me help you. That's brave. You've made it through everything."

"I haven't told you everything." And Sam hadn't asked. I was glad, because I wasn't sure I was ready to tell him the last thing—the big thing. "I don't feel brave."

"Maybe being brave isn't about how you

194

feel; it's about doing what needs to be done, despite what you feel."

The sound of someone shouting filtered into the office. I remembered this wasn't our normal night. "I should get going. I told Connie I wouldn't be long. I just needed to see you."

Sam took my hand in his. I noticed how nicely they fit together. "I'm always here for you, Lex. Not just Mondays, any day, any time."

"I know that, Sam. That's why I came."

I left Sam to his Friday-night crowd and went back to the cottage.

Being able to lean on someone else . . . maybe that was brave. I mean, if you leaned on someone, you had to trust that they wouldn't let you fall.

After everything, I could still trust. I trusted my kids enough to share tonight with them. I trusted my mom—she'd have come if I'd called.

And I trusted Sam. I trusted in the healing power of our Monday nights, and our one-things.

I drove the snow-covered road home. The snow had stopped and the clouds had momentarily cleared. A half-moon illuminated the fields, then disappeared as I entered the wood-lined section of road that led to the cottage.

I felt centered. Eased. Letting go of the Erie house was another step in my healing.

And after talking to Sam, I felt braver than I'd felt in a very long time.

Chapter Nineteen

Connie left the next morning to drive back to Cleveland. I was thankful it had stopped snowing. She planned on renting a U-Haul when she came back in a couple weeks for Christmas.

After she left, I stared at the pile of things I'd brought from the house. Lee's ugly red sweater was on the top of the heap. Rather than put the things away, Angus and I trudged through the snow to the barn. I brought the sweater with me.

I tossed it on the back of the couch, then I lit the fire in the cast-iron stove. It didn't take long for the room to warm up enough for me to take off my coat.

I stared at the loom.

I needed to finish the piece, but in order to do it, I'd have to face my last big thing and I wasn't sure I was ready, but I knew I had to. Maybe Sam was right; being brave wasn't so much feeling brave as it was doing what needed to be done.

I walked back over to the couch and picked up the sweater, fingering the wool.

I remembered Lee laughing as I complained

about how ratty it looked. He'd put it on and grin as he waited for my anticipated complaints. It became a joke between us.

But I also remembered other times he wore the sweater. Times that brought no jokes or smiles.

I smelled the sweater, burying my face deep in its rough warmth. I could have sworn it still smelled of Lee's cologne.

I went to my workbench and took out scissors and before I could second-guess myself, I clipped a seam and started to unravel the yarn. Slowly, I pulled a long piece of the red wool out. Then I sat at the loom. I knew what I needed to weave next, just as I knew what my next one-thing had to be. I called Sam. "I know Saturdays are busy and that we meet Monday nights, but I need to tell you this one-thing alone." An urgency to finish pressed on me, and I was on the verge of asking him to get someone to cover at the bar, but in the end, I didn't ask.

I didn't have to.

"I'll get Chris to cover." There was no hesitation, no complaint, just Sam saying, "Should we meet at your place?"

No. I didn't want to bring this particular one-thing here and I couldn't take it to the bar. This one needed privacy. "Could we meet somewhere else—somewhere that we won't be overheard?"

"Do you care what time?"

"No."

"I'll pick you up around three."

"Thanks, Sam."

I kept glancing at the loom, but I didn't work on the tapestry. I didn't work on glazing my bowl. I simply sat next to Angus on the couch and unraveled Lee's sweater. I purposefully tried not to think, not to remember. I'd do that later with Sam.

About one, Angus and I trudged through the snow, back to the cottage. I made sure he had food and water, then forced myself to eat some soup, not because I was hungry, but because I knew I should be hungry.

I showered, dressed, and was waiting for Sam when he pulled up.

"Thank you, again," I said by way of greeting.

He nodded. We didn't say much on the drive. I wasn't sure where we were going, but I didn't ask.

Sam drove down I-79, then into Erie and to the peninsula. He parked at one of the lookout points on the bay side. The water hadn't frozen over yet, but it looked thicker to me. Like a greyish snow cone. As if with just one or two more freezing nights the bay's water might turn to ice.

I could see the city across from us. The tall tower at the end of the pier.

"I thought this would be private," he said. "Neutral ground."

Sitting in Sam's truck there was no chance we'd be overheard. To be honest, in the winter, the peninsula was quiet enough that we didn't even see another car.

"Thanks, Sam." I was quiet a few minutes, trying to formulate this one-thing. Most of the time, the stories just spilled out. This one was premeditated. "Before we do this, I need you to understand that Lee was a good dad."

Sam nodded, not saying anything.

I kept going, needing to be sure he believed it, not just believed me. "There are so many examples. The kids were maybe fourteen and thirteen when we had that huge snowstorm. It knocked out power to our house for two days. Rather than fret about things melting in the freezer, or missed appointments, Lee lit candles and announced we were going to have an eat-the-food-before-it-spoils picnic while we played the world's longest game of Scrabble. We had two games, an old one with missing tiles, and a new one we'd just bought. He duct-taped the boards together, combined the tiles, and we played all night. It sounds like such a little thing, but the kids still talk about the Scrabble storm. That was the thing about Lee—he could make anything an adventure."

Sam sat on his side of the truck, nodding, not saying anything because he knew I needed to do this–this one-thing, one big thing, was the elephant in the room. I'd danced around it, circumventing it. It was the one-thing that was the straw . . . my straw.

"Even when they were little, the kids loved him. My story with them was Belinda Mae, because I could sing and Lee, like my grandmother before him, couldn't hit a note if it were the broadside of a barn. But he was better at the rest of the books. He could make the stories come alive in a way I never could. When they were little, he'd do Sendak's *Where the Wild Things Are* and have the kids gnashing along with him. When it was good, he was very good."

Sam finally broke his silence. "And when it wasn't good?"

I didn't answer right away. The weight of this one-thing was hard to get out from under.

"This is it," Sam stated. "This is what all your one-things were leading to. My shrink would say those other things were tests."

"Tests?"

"To see if you could trust me. Sharing things that mattered, but not the big thing that had you leave your home in Erie and sent you out to the woods."

"You have a shrink?"

Sam nodded. "Had. PTSD. There was Grid, but I needed more, especially when he left. It wasn't the injury that immobilized me in the hospital. And it wasn't the injuries that haunted my dreams. It was the weight of the memories. I'd wake up from a dream—they were always so real that I'd have to check to be sure I wasn't really covered in blood. Even in my dream I'd know that my best attempts wouldn't be good enough." He looked down at his hand, as if expecting to see it covered in blood. "I was trained to save people. I was that kid in school who always had As. I excelled. I wasn't prepared to fail. I especially wasn't trained to fail on such an epic level. I was trained to be sure and decisive—I was trained to save."

"Trained?"

"I was a doctor."

The four words sank in. Sam hadn't gone to fight; he'd gone to heal. His job had been to save people. He'd been trained to fix people.

"When I was younger, I thought I'd play in the NBA. My best friend, Neil, and I had it all planned out. We'd both play college ball, then move to the big leagues. But when

I was a sophomore in high school, everything changed."

❧

"Neil," Sam screamed as he raised his arms, calling for the ball.

Neil passed it to him and Sam shot his best friend a look. He knew that Neil was ready. They'd practiced this play for weeks. Sam set up the shot, and Neil sprinted toward the hoop. Sam threw the ball upward in front of Neil, who jumped, caught it and was ready to sink it into the basket, when number eight from the other team jumped as well, slamming into Neil midair.

Sam watched as Neil fell. It felt as if it happened in slow motion. His best friend, still clutching the ball, fell toward the floor. Number eight plucked the ball out of Neil's arms.

The sound of Neil's head hitting the hardwood reverberated through the auditorium. But no one but Sam seemed to notice. Everyone else was focused on number eight as he sprinted toward the other team's hoop with the rest of Sam's team hot on his heels.

Normally, Sam would be running after him, too, trusting that Neil would climb to his feet and follow.

But there was something that kept him stationary under the net. He looked at Neil, who hadn't moved or opened his eyes.

Then his best friend started to convulse.

And still Sam stood there, watching Neil jerk so hard that his head hit the floor again.

Sam didn't know what to do.

He barely registered that the ref blew his whistle. The coaches ran onto the floor and the players stood under the other team's net, watching as Neil moved spastically.

Sam didn't know what to do to help.

He stood frozen as the paramedics arrived and took the still unconscious Neil away on a stretcher.

☙

"I can still see it all so clearly in my mind. From that moment on, I knew that I'd never play in the NBA. That dream gave way to another. I would be a doctor. I'd never again not know what to do. That's what I thought, at least. I told myself that if I'd been a doctor, I could have saved Neil. In my mind, I'd save everyone. But that's not what happened. I couldn't save everyone. I couldn't even save myself."

I reached out and took his hand.

All the things he'd told me, they'd been tests as well, I realized. "I'm sorry about Neil. After Gracie died, my mom said that sometimes you can't save everyone. Sometimes it's okay to simply save yourself. No matter what you say, you did save me. Before you, I survived. But surviving isn't living. I'd gone through the motions until I walked into your bar. You saved me, Sam. I'm alive again because of you. I want to save you, too."

"So tonight we do our one big thing?" he asked.

I nodded. "One-thing with you has become my absolution. No, that's after confession, when the priest absolves you. Our one-things are my permission to let go and move on. Somewhere along the line, I recognized that."

"And there's one more thing you need to move on from," he said. Slowly, recognizing the significance, Sam said the words. "One thing?"

"I think there are tipping points in recovery. Points when things get better or sometimes worse. Sometimes there are a lot of tipping points as you heal—new levels as you try to rediscover yourself. But some moments are more than tipping points. They're more like lines. You don't always recognize it as you approach, but you can see it in hindsight. You cross that line; then everything's different. You're different. My father's death was a line like that."

"How did you change?"

"I discovered he wasn't perfect. I found my mother's laughter and realized how much she loved me. That kind of knowledge can't help but change you. I was different after that."

"And Gracie?"

"That's a pain I'll never fully get over, but I learned to live again. I learned to appreciate Connie and Conner. I guess I grew up."

"And . . ."

"And I thought I'd faced the worst of it. But there was Lee. You haven't asked what happened to him."

"I knew you'd tell me when you were ready."

"He died."

"I'm sorry."

Sitting in the truck, staring out at the ever-darkening bay, I realized I was too. I was sorry about Lee.

"But there's more. You see, as I've told you these things, I never told you about Lee. That's why I needed to tell you that he was a good father. He had very big highs, but he paid for it with very deep lows. When I met him, that day on campus, he was on a high. When he went low, I was there to pull him out. After Gracie, he went low. I did, too. I could barely save myself, much less pull him out of his depression. There was a whole other depth to Lee's lows. Medication helped even things out, but he didn't always stay on it."

"After the kids graduated . . ." Sam prompted.

"We got back together and took the trip to Ireland. Things were good for a while. For a few years. Then he went off his meds. I realized it one night when . . ."

Lexie pulled in the garage and was happy to see Lee's car there. She couldn't wait to share her news. Maybe that's the secret to a good marriage—having someone you want to share your good news with. She'd been asked to enter some of her pottery in a local exhibit. "Lee," she called as she came in, hung her coat on the hook, and kicked off her shoes. "We're going out to dinner. You'll never guess . . ."

The house was dark. There was no sound.

"Lee," she called again. Still nothing.

She wandered through the house, looking in each room. She went upstairs and checked the bedrooms, one by one. She paused outside Gracie's door, then forced herself to twist the handle and go in.

Lee lay curled up in a fetal position on her bed, facing the wall.

"Lee?"

"It's not helping, Lex." He didn't turn around as he spoke. Didn't move. "I thought if we got back together, I'd feel better. I'd feel like myself again. But I don't. I thought you might be enough, but you're not."

His words cut at her, but she forced herself to put the pain on hold. "Did you take your meds today?"

"They don't help. They just make everything fuzzy. I feel numb."

"Maybe numb is better than this."

"You're not my mother, Lex. Hell, I don't even think you're going to be my wife much longer. We should have just stayed divorced."

"Lee, this is your illness talking."

"No, this is me. Me off the medications. Me allowing myself to feel. And right now, I feel as if I was wrong to get back together with you. I was wrong to think we could get back what we had. It's over. We're over."

"Fine. We can be over after you get better. Why don't I take you to the hospital? Remember how much better you felt last time?"

Lee finally turned and faced her. She hardly recognized him. His face was etched with despair as keen as it had been right after Gracie.

"Don't you think I'd go with you if I thought it would help? It won't. Nothing will help."

"You stay here, and I'll go call Conner."

"No. I don't want him to see me like this."

Lee lived under the delusion that the kids didn't know he was sick. "He's seen you like this before," she reminded him gently. "He'd want to help."

As if he'd used up all his energy, Lee turned back to the wall.

Lexie wanted to cry. She knew it was Lee's illness talking, but knowing and feeling were two different things, and right now, she was feeling hurt.

For so many years she'd overlooked moments like these. She told herself Lee couldn't help his illness. He couldn't help the words he threw at her like weapons. They were designed to hurt her. To make her feel the pain that he felt.

Well, he'd done that. His words hurt.

But rather than being crushed by the pain of it, she was angry.

She'd felt many things about Lee. Love. Amusement. Gratitude. Sadness. But for the first time, she was well and truly angry.

⚬

"I thought you might be enough, but you're not." I sighed. "I knew it was his illness, and I knew he loved me. But those words hurt. And for the first time, I didn't want to make allowances for his illness. He'd hurt me because he could and I was angry."

"What happened then?"

"Conner came and helped me get Lee to the hospital. We checked him into the psych ward. They started his meds again and he went to his therapist, but those words stood between us. He apologized and I said it was okay, but it wasn't. I wasn't enough. I hadn't been enough to save Gracie. I wasn't enough to save Lee. He was slipping and I couldn't hold on to him. I tried. I'd healed enough from losing Gracie that I thought I could help him, like I always had. But after we took him to the hospital, things got worse. A year and a half ago . . .

Lexie woke up with what the kids used to call brain-fuzz. It took her a moment to orient herself to where and when she was. The where was pretty easy—in bed. The when was a bit harder—she glanced at the clock and it read three. Three in the morning, she quickly determined. The next thing that filtered through her fuzz was that she was in the bed alone. Lee wasn't there.

After that, the realization that someone was ringing the doorbell made it through.

It was probably Lee.

She couldn't decide why he'd be out until three in the morning and was still too fuzzy to figure it out. She'd let him in and just ask.

She didn't bother with slippers or a robe. Lee had seen her in her scruffy cutoff sweats and tank-top pajamas before.

She opened the door and started to say, "Where were—" She didn't get to the *you* part because it wasn't Lee at the door. It was a police officer.

A police officer wearing a very pained expression. He probably knew Conner. She wondered if something had happened to her son. "Mrs. McCain?"

"Yes. Is it Conner?"

The cop looked confused.

"My son's a cop," she explained.

She saw the recognition in his eyes. He shook his head. "No, I'm not here about a Conner. Maybe I should call him and—"

Suddenly, Lexie knew. "It's about my husband?"

He nodded. "Your husband is Julian McCain?"

"Lee. He hated being called Julian." She said the words, even though she knew Lee's preferences didn't matter anymore. The police officer didn't need to say another word, because she knew. It was easier to comment on his name than on the fact that Lee was gone.

She wasn't sure how, but she knew her husband was gone.

<hr/>

"The cop called Conner. He showed up fifteen minutes later. They said it was an accident. I'd like to believe it was, but I can't. Lee wouldn't take his meds and had been so depressed. I'd never seen him that bad before."

After that last time in the hospital, I brought him home and his mood had evened out for a few weeks, but then got worse. "He lost his job. He'd be in bed when I went to work, and he'd still be there when I got home. I couldn't pull him from this hole and neither could the kids. In fact, after they would visit, he'd be worse, so they stopped visiting. I think it was all just too much. I think he . . ." I hesitated. I'd never given voice to the thought before. "I think he killed himself. I think he drove his car into the side of the hill."

"Lex . . ."

"I was used to his highs and lows, but this wasn't just low. He'd fallen down the rabbit hole and no amount of therapy or medication seemed to help."

I realized Sam was holding my hand as he squeezed it. "Lex, I'm so sorry."

"So am I. I wanted to save him, but I couldn't."

"You talked about a line," Sam said. "Something you don't recognize until afterwards. This was your line. This is why you moved out to the cottage, isn't it?"

"Yes. And before, I figured out who I was after I crossed a line—after Gracie and my dad. But I've floundered since losing Lee. Since he left me. I've been sad, but I've been angry, too. I've been so much of both, I haven't had time to figure out who I am now."

"I know who you are. I could tell you, but telling doesn't work. You have to figure it out on your own. You have to know in your heart that you did everything you could for Lee. And maybe you need to face the fact you can't save everyone. You can love them, but you can't save them. No matter how much you want to, you can't."

Sam got very quiet. He looked blindsided.

I sat with him, waiting, and finally he whispered, "You can't save everyone. I crossed a line after I came home and I think I just now figured out who I am on this side of it."

He squeezed my hand. "I couldn't save Neil. He died that night from traumatic brain injury. I couldn't help but feel guilty. If we hadn't worked on the play, if he hadn't gone for that shot . . . I lost my best friend. I became a doctor and thought I could make it up to Neil by saving others. I thought that I could do that in the military, so I volunteered. And . . ."

He stopped. Waiting. Waiting for the words that would allow him to share.

"One thing," I said.

He got quiet again and then said, "I don't remember the explosion. I just remember the aftermath."

⚭

Sam returned to awareness slowly.

He breathed in air so dry it felt grainy in his nose.

Then he registered a smell. Something petroleum. And hot. No, heat didn't smell. He felt heat. His body felt sticky with sweat in the heat.

He was Sam Corner.

Dr. Sam Corner.

Aware that he had a patient. They were transporting . . .

He couldn't quite put his finger on where they were going, only that they were going and he had a patient. His head ached with a pressure that seemed to be growing by the minute.

He opened his eyes and tried to figure out what was going on. He was looking at what must be the sky, but it was pink and crackled.

It took time to figure out that he was staring through a shattered windshield, and the pink hue was due to blood. Blood all over the windshield.

He raised his hand to his forehead and as he moved, pain hit, radiating from his leg. Excruciating.

"Ramsey? Grid? Lyle?"

No one answered. At least he thought no one answered. His voice had sounded odd to his own ear.

And, despite the unremitting pain, that's when it all came together.

A bomb. An explosion. It's why his leg hurt, why his ears were messed up.

It might be why no one else in the transport was answering.

He pulled himself from his seat, his leg screaming with each movement.

He saw Lennon, Smith, and Johnson. He didn't

need his medical degree to know they weren't coming back.

Then he saw a body through the back of the vehicle, which was somewhere around where the middle of the vehicle had once been. He crawled through the wreckage and saw his patient, Ramsey. He saw his chest rise slightly.

Disregarding the pain, he flung himself down onto the ground and started CPR.

♋

"It was too late. I couldn't save him either. I don't know how long I did compressions. I don't remember the medics coming and prying me away from his body, though they tell me they did. I don't remember much. The bleeding in my brain got worse and soon I was out. I didn't wake up again until I was back in Pittsburgh. What haunted me when I woke up was that I couldn't save them. Grid made it, but not because of anything I did."

"You tried, Sam. Maybe that has to be enough." He looked at me. We'd become close enough that I could read his expression. "Maybe it has to be enough for both of us."

He wrapped me in his arms without saying anything.

I'm not sure how much time went by, but later, he said, "Thank you. I didn't know how much I needed to hear someone say that until you said it."

I repeated myself, more because I needed to hear myself say the words again. An audible musing. "Life is full of lines that you don't know you've crossed until you're on the other side. And once you're there, you need to discover who you're going to be. I think both of us made a great start at putting our past behind us, and we're figuring out who we are now. All that's left is deciding what we want for our future."

"I know one thing about my future . . . I want you in it."

I nodded against his chest. "Same here."

"Well, then I guess that's more than enough for one night."

It was dark now. Western Pennsylvania gets dark early in December. Erie might not be a big city, but it was big enough that it gradually lit up across the bay as the sky got darker. As if on cue, a light flashed behind us and one of the park's rangers got out and walked up to Sam's window.

Sam unrolled it. "Sorry, Officer. I know it's after hours. We were just leaving."

The man took a flashlight and skimmed it along the inside of the truck. I don't know what he saw, but he simply nodded. "Sometimes time gets away from all of us. Good night, folks."

He got back in his car and waited until

we pulled out and headed out of the park.

"Sam," I said from my side of the truck. "Would you stay with me tonight?"

He reached across the expanse and took my hand in his. "I thought you'd never ask."

Chapter Twenty

I woke up the next morning sandwiched between Sam and Angus.

Both were bed-hogs.

I was debating about which one to climb over to get out of the bed, when Sam said, "Good morning."

I kissed his cheek. "I'm sorry I woke you."

"You didn't. I've been awake for a while now, thinking."

"About?"

"About Lee, about what you told me last night. I don't think it matters if Lee's accident wasn't an accident."

"Don't you see; I don't know if the accident was an accident, or if he—"

"It doesn't matter," he reiterated.

"It does. If he did it on purpose, it's one thing that might break me." And I'd never know. The uncertainty ate at me. "If it was an accident, I could mourn. I'd find my way back, but if it wasn't . . ."

He reached up and stroked my cheek with his hand. "We've been wrong—you and I. All wrong."

"I don't understand."

Sam sat up in bed, and the sheet dipped low, exposing his chest. And despite last night, I wanted him again. Making love to Sam was easier than talking. "One thing."

I shook my head. I couldn't share one-thing with him. I'd already given him the biggest one and he was telling me I was wrong. Suddenly I was pissed. "No more, Sam. Make love to me if you want. Have breakfast with me. Or go if you must. But I can't share anything else with you now. You've never told me I was wrong before. You've never judged my feelings. And now you want me to share more with you? No." I shook my head. "No."

"No, I wasn't asking for you to share; I was stating. Your feelings weren't wrong. Our assumptions were. We've shared our lives with each other one thing at a time. We've shared week after week. One thing after one thing because we both intuitively knew that just one thing can never be the measure of someone's life. One thing is . . . well, it's just that. It's one thing. Even if Lee did mean it—if he committed suicide—and it wasn't an accident, it was his illness speaking and that's just one part of who he was. His illness was just one part of Lee McCain. Maybe it's significant that you told me so many other things about him first. He loved you. He loved

219

the kids and was a good father. He knew how to laugh. He read to his children. I know him through your memories, through the family he left behind, but I know that he was more than just that last moment of his life. He was more than his illness."

My anger evaporated and I sobbed. There were no silent tears, no crying leading up to it, just a swift, immediate sob.

And I remembered.

Lee on the quad, the day we met.

Singing so off-key to Gracie when she was young.

Bumming around the house in his awful red sweater.

Jokingly swatting my behind in Ireland.

Buying me a Guinness and comforting me.

Pictures of Lee flitted through my mind, like a slide show. One thing after another.

Lee was more than just one of them. He was more than any one of them. I could never really know what happened in that last moment, but if he did . . .

Well, if he did die on purpose, he was more than that.

His life was more than that.

I sat a moment by Sam and I suddenly knew what I needed to do next. "Sam, I'm going to church this morning. Want to come?"

He gave me a searching look, then nodded.

"Sure. Although, I should warn you, I haven't been to church in a long time."

"Neither have I," I told him. "Maybe that's part of this side of that line we just crossed. We're on the other side now and it's time to go back."

An hour later, we walked up the snow-covered road to the small church I'd gone to with my family when the kids were young—the church I'd passed so often. The music hadn't started yet and cars were pulling into the parking lot. I stood there a minute, locked in indecision.

"Are you sure you want to do this, Lex?"

"I'm sure I do; I'm just not sure how God feels about that."

"I'm obviously no expert, but I think that's the one thing about God . . . the door's always open. You just need to walk through it. I don't think God needed either of us to figure out who we were on the other side of the line—he's known all along and was just waiting."

Sam took my hand and we went into the church. There was a woman at the back, greeting people as they came in. "You're new," she said with a quick smile of acceptance. "Welcome. I'm Jane."

"Lexie," I leaned toward Sam, "and Sam."

Jane led us into the church, and as if sensing our nervousness, she found us a pew midway in. Not so far to the front as to call attention to ourselves, and not so far in the back to make us feel unwelcome.

An elderly man with wild white hair opened the service with a song and the congregation followed. Then he walked to the small pulpit and said, "Today's reading is, Luke, chapter nine, verse eleven. 'And the people, when they knew it, followed him: and he received them, and spake unto them of the kingdom of God, and healed them that had need of healing.' "

I squeezed Sam's hand and he squeezed mine back. I felt as if the pastor spoke to me. I'd been in need of healing and hadn't even known it, and then I'd wandered into The Corner Bar, not so much for a beer, but to connect with people. To feel part of something, even if I'd only planned on staying on the fringes.

Week after week, I'd sat there at the edges, until Sam asked, "One thing?" and that simple question had changed everything. At one point Sam had said something about healing despite himself. I realized that I'd healed despite myself, too.

"I believe," the pastor was saying, "that people come into our lives for a reason. When we need them. They are gifts . . ."

I squeezed Sam's hand again. He was a

gift. He'd helped me find myself again. He'd helped me find my way back to here . . . to church.

I'd been so mad at God. I'd seen all the things I lost, not the things I had.

Gracie said that she'd rather have a few years with us than longer with anyone else. I thought of the people I'd lost. I wouldn't give up a minute I had with any of them. And the journey I'd taken had led me here. Sitting next to Sam in church.

I was right. There were lines in life, and when Lee had died, I'd crossed another one. And now, on the other side, I finally found out who I was. I knew in my heart who I was, and where I was meant to be.

After the service, church members and the minister came over and greeted us, inviting us back. I smiled and thanked him as I assured him I'd be back.

When Sam and I walked back to the cottage, I told him, "I'm going to take Monday off. I have something I need to finish. But would you come to dinner Christmas Eve? Mom and the kids will be here. I have something I need to show everyone who matters to me."

He kissed me. "I'll be there. Lex, I need to tell you that—"

"Tell me after I show you one more thing on

Christmas Eve. Once I've done that, I'll have something to tell you as well."

He nodded, accepting my choice, accepting me.

When he left, Angus and I went to the workshop. I started a fire, picked up the skein of red wool that had once been Lee's sweater, and got down to work. I knew how the tapestry should be finished.

Chapter Twenty-One

I worked to finish the tapestry. It was as if I couldn't completely be on the other side of the line until it was done.

I talked to Sam on the phone every day, but I didn't go to the bar and I didn't invite him to my house. I needed time to assimilate everything.

Instead, I wove.

When you're weaving, the warp are the stationary threads that are held under tension. The weft are the threads you weave in and out of the warp. In traditional weaving, you see the warp and weft. When making a tapestry, the weaver hides the warp beneath the weft.

When I think tapestry, I think huge hangings on some castle wall. Scenes of kings and queens, maybe a unicorn or two.

My completed piece would be more like a quilt, small block pictures with a very impressionistic feel.

Five feet wide, seven feet long.

Pictures bordered by dusky-blue, traditional weaving, warp and weft both visible.

I finished the last image, and then finished the piece with a foot of regular weaving.

There was something calming about the order of it. Using my foot, I depressed the treadle, which lifted half of the warp threads, creating a shed I pushed the shuttle through. I battened the yarn down, compressing it against the finished cloth, then raised the other half of the warp, passed the shuttle through . . .

There was a certainty to this. When I'd created pictures, it had been free-form and each square had been highly individual. The resulting patches were very impressionistic pictures. The border was uniform and orderly, comforting in the rhythm of it.

Treadle, shuttle, batten.

Treadle, shuttle, batten.

The weft moved between the warp, tying everything together. Binding the pieces into a whole.

I finished the tapestry and took it inside the cottage. I tried to decide where to put it, and ultimately hung it over the fireplace. Months of my life had been spent working on this tapestry. It was imperfect, sure, but then so was my life. I sat on the couch, studying the piece.

I thought of the story that the Amish always put an imperfection in their quilts because only God is perfect. Maybe that's wrong.

Maybe they put a flaw in their quilts because

those imperfections are what make us who and what we are.

Our imperfections help define us as surely as our strengths.

I had finished the piece and knew that I had completely and finally moved to the other side of the line.

And I knew who I was.

Chapter Twenty-Two

I awoke on Christmas Eve morning feeling a childlike anticipation. Angus nuzzled my face, telling me he needed to go outside. He romped around the snow-covered woods while I started coffee. Angus returned, smelling of wet dog and waiting for his food.

I filled his bowl, took a cup of coffee, and went into the living room. I turned on the Christmas tree lights, then studied the tapestry hanging over the fireplace.

I spent the day getting ready for my Christmas Eve guests. Connie was coming down from Cleveland and spending the next four days with me. My mother and Conner were driving in from Erie in the afternoon, and Sam would arrive around the same time.

I cleaned and cooked. And when it was all ready, I sat down with Angus and simply enjoyed the festive look of the house.

Angus heard the first car to pull in. It was Sam. I kissed his cheek. "Merry Christmas, Sam."

"Merry Christmas, Lexie."

We waited in the kitchen and within an hour the kids and my mother arrived. "Before we eat, I want to show you what I've been working on since summer."

I led them to the living room and pointed at my perfectly imperfect weaving.

"It will never win any awards," I said. "But I spent the better part of the year working on it." My mother, the kids, and Sam all studied it. Even Angus, sitting on the couch, seemed to be studying it.

I stared at it along with them, each of the pictures representing moments in my life and the lines I'd crossed without even realizing it until some time after. Rows and columns of one-things.

"Sam finally helped me understand the tapestry . . . more than that, he made me understand myself and my life."

"Understand what, Mom?" Connie asked.

It was time to tell the kids my story. "I moved out here because I was hurt. Your father, right before he died, was going through another bad time."

Connie and Conner both nodded. They had lived through their father's bad times. "I know the police said his accident was an accident, but I wasn't so sure. And that not knowing, the worrying that maybe he'd hurt himself because I hadn't been able to save him . . . Well, it did me in."

"Mom," Connie said for both herself and

her twin, even as my mother said, "Alexis."

They hugged me, and I was wrapped in family, gaining strength from them, from their love. "I was lost, until Sam. He asked me to share one thing with him. At first I told him my name, and other small things, but gradually, I told him bigger things, and he taught me something profound."

I looked at Sam Corner, a man who had his own baggage and was learning to deal with it. "Sam taught me that your dad was more than just one thing. He was more than what he did or didn't do in those last moments. He was a compilation of many things. Many moments.

"He was brilliant, funny, driven, and sometimes . . ."

"Very sad," Conner supplied.

I nodded. "Those sad moments, his last moment . . . he was more than that. I made this tapestry to show the moments in my life. The important moments."

I pointed to the squares. "Mom, showing me you knew how to laugh, and how much you loved me. You kids, graduating. Your sister's love of horses. All these represent something or someone—they represent one thing that has made me who I am. But I'm more than any of these big moments. I think I'm more the smaller ones. I am peanut butter sandwiches with you kids on a rainy Saturday afternoon.

I am Scrabble games in a storm. I'm the mom who read you *Belinda Mae*, or scolded you for climbing on the garage roof. I am Sunday mornings at church—"

Connie caught on. "You are the one who held me when Brian Miller broke my heart."

Conner nodded. "You are the one who taught me to drive because Dad wasn't as good at it as he thought he'd be."

My mother reached out and took my hand. "You are my daughter and you taught me how to express my feelings," she grinned, "well, at least to express them better than I used to."

Sam looked at me and smiled. He leaned in and whispered in my ear, "You are the woman I want to spend the rest of my life with."

I'd crossed another line. A big line. A good line.

Surrounded by my family, we shared dinner and a holiday. We played Christmas Scrabble, a family version that allows only words that are in some Christmas carol, or can be used in a sentence about Christmas. I still maintain that threnody—a song of lamentation—was a cheat. I mean, Sam's sentence was, "The Christmas carol was the antithesis of the threnody I sang last month." That's not a very Christmasy word, but then I realized that my whole last year had been a threnody of sorts and that *Joy to the World* was definitely the antithesis of it, because there, arguing about a Scrabble word with Sam in front of the Christmas tree, with my mother and kids nearby . . . it was definitely joy.

Epilogue

The Other Side of the Line

I hate it when stories end without really sharing the rest. This is a memoir of sorts, but there's so much more to my life. So many more one-things I've added to my tapestry of my life since this story ended.

We're building a life, Sam, Angus, and me. I'm teaching again. Not at the school, but lessons at my workshop. Basket weaving. Pottery. Basic drawing lessons. I don't teach weaving because I don't know enough. I don't know that I'll ever weave another thing, but I've kept the loom. I hope that Lee knows what a gift it had been. That one piece—my tapestry—was as important to my healing as Sam and our one-things.

I still go to the bar on Mondays, and Sam, he comes home to me each night when it closes.

Chris, Sam's new bartender, has been working more, which means on Saturdays, Sam has time to run a free clinic. He spent time jumping through the licensing hoops and more to pay for his insurance. He's not ready

233

to practice medicine again full-time, but he realizes his knowledge is a gift that shouldn't be squandered because of old memories. One thing can't stop the doctor in him. I work as his receptionist and assistant on those Saturday clinic days. Angus comes and sleeps on the floor. He seems to comfort the patients as much as he comforted me.

On Sundays, we both go to church down the street. Sometimes the kids or Mom come along. I sing hymns and listen to Reverend Bob. We've become part of the church community there and it has become an important part of our lives. Reverend Bob asked if I'd consider working with the youth group, supervising them as they paint a mural in the church basement, which serves as our gathering center. I said yes, so I am once again surrounded by kids and teens. It's loud, and don't even get me started about when Brian Langard spilled the paint down Eric Roberts's pants. And last week, I caught a small cluster of kids discussing climbing the rope for the church bell. My thoughts immediately turned to the kids on the garage roof.

That made me wonder about the house in Erie. I went to Conner's for dinner one night and drove by it. The lights were on in the living room. I'll confess, I parked a bit up the road, then walked back and stood on the sidewalk, looking in at a family. Two adults and two children.

They seemed happy.

The house was now filling with their story, their memories, one thing at a time.

I walked away and haven't driven up the street again since.

My life is good and getting better.

I know I will suffer other losses, but I can trust that I will mourn and recover. I know there will be other lines and tipping points. That things will happen. But I'm sure I'll be fine because I realize now that I am always evolving—always becoming more. And I know that we're all more than just one thing.

That I'm more than one thing.

That Sam's more than one thing.

And maybe the one true thing is that together we are so much more than we are apart.

Sometimes the journey to forgiving your-self—to finding yourself—starts with one person, one step . . . with just one thing.

And I think now you have the real end of my story.

A happily-most-of-the-time sort of ending.

~Lexie Corner

Note from the Author

When I was in school, my English teacher Ms. Mac always asked, "So what was the author trying to say?" I maintained that sometimes the author wasn't trying to "say" anything, but was simply trying to tell a good story. As a writer, sometimes I simply tell a story and then, much to my chagrin, I find I was indeed trying to say something. And then I discover, what I was trying to say wasn't always what I thought I was trying to say.

For instance, in *Just One Thing*, when I realized I was saying something, I thought it was *you can recover after something bad happens*. It's a simple message. I thought I was trying to say that life is like weaving, *it's up and it's down. You just need to ride the weft until you come back out on top.*

As I finished Sam and Lexie's story, I discovered that what I really said was, *a person's life can't be defined by one incident.* We are the whole of our experiences. We are the warp, and life is the weft, going up and down around us, transforming us in its wake. Each new line adds to the whole . . . adds to our strength. I think Ms. Mac would have liked the "message."

But really, as a writer, I started to tell a story about pain, about healing, about love . . . and hey, even about Guinness. Yes, I do love the stuff! I hope you enjoyed Lexie and Sam's story.

About the Author

Award-winning author Holly Jacobs has sold over two million books worldwide. The first novel in her *Everything But . . .* series, *Everything But a Groom*, was named one of 2008's Best Romances by *Booklist*, and her books have been honored with many other accolades.

Holly has a wide range of interests, from her love for writing to gardening and even basket weaving. She has delivered more than sixty author workshops and keynote speeches across the country. She lives in Erie, Pennsylvania, with her family and her dogs. She frequently sets stories in and around her hometown.

Center Point Large Print
600 Brooks Road / PO Box 1
Thorndike, ME 04986-0001 USA

(207) 568-3717

US & Canada:
1 800 929-9108
www.centerpointlargeprint.com